May December Come Gently

JoMikDo

MAY DECEMBER COME GENTLY

Yamazakura – the Wild Cherry Blossom

JoMikDo

Osaka Road

Wild cherry blossoms lightly gave up precious petals to the gentle breeze as warm ethereal hands sent a shower of pink and white autumn snow down upon the child's face, brushing against her soft cheeks. Each burst of petals loosened by the wind brought a squeal of delight and a pirouette from the tiny, exuberant child.

A woman's voice called out her name.

She looked in the direction of the voice. There, in the dirt path, which led from the house to her wild cherry tree, a woman, stood partially obscured by a thick shower of soft petals. Beyond the woman, she scarcely made out the pale figure of a man standing in the distance.

"Mommy!" the girl's joyous voice rang out, reverberating off trees and the house with a sharp snap, passing into an echo, which faded back into dead silence. The little girl ran to the arms of her mother, who stooped over to scoop her up. She hugged the woman's neck, kissing her cheek. The woman carried the contented girl towards the house. Walking past the man and up to the open door, she put the child down, turned around and walked away.

The girl's smile departed with her mother as mystified dread overcame her. Confused, she softly called out to her mother, "Mommy? Where are you going?"

The silent woman kept walking until she strolled near the man. He reached out and took her hand and walked off with her.

She called out all the louder, "Where are you going mommy? Is that my daddy? Please come back!"

The little girl moved one foot forward as if to follow the couple but felt the piercing grip of hooked fingers cut into her shoulders. The woman and the man turned back towards her. Their faces were blank—they had neither nose, nor eyes, nor mouth—they were featureless. Terror ran up the child's spine like a firework.

She gazed back over her shoulder to see whom it was gripping at her shoulders. A dark hand, which seemed more shadow than flesh, gripped her upper arm. Her eyes followed the dark arms back into the abyss of the door's portal. The arms were extensions of the darkness itself, so black, so deep that all light, all consciousness were being sucked into it.

Her parents faded into the distance. She turned to call out, but shadow hands gagged her. The child was pulled violently back into the darkness; the only sound was a sudden and final clap of the shutting door – like the lid of a coffin being sealed.

A vibration tickled Suki's cheek, while just beyond her

eyelids the light was growing dim and then brighter. She forced her eyes open. Relieving the oppression of the recurring dream.

Her head, lying sideways on open books, gave the impression that the library study hall was on its side. The bright, white fluorescent light from the study table's common desk lamp dimmed again which caused her to blink a few times before picking up the cell phone – that had been vibrating on the desk next to her face – to checked the time.

"Ten forty-five?" She squinted at the time again. "Ten forty-five!" Her head jolted upright as she stared at her phone. "It must be broken." Suki looked at the clock on the far wall that confirmed the late hour. She also confirmed two text messages and a voice mail from her roommate Michiko.

The first message time coded at 18.18 said: *Me n Kuno goin 2 karaoke. Drop books and join us :)*

It was followed by Suki's curt reply at 18:20: *U said we'd study 2gether for the mock exam tomorrow :(*

Sory wl cram w/u l8r 2nyt OK? Kuno's buying ;)

Suki did not reply. She was upset, but she did not want to annoy her flighty roommate and the only close friend she had made since coming to Tokyo to study.

The last message was coded at 22:15: *On way bak now. Wil beet curfew :~o.*

"Oh no, the dorm curfew!" Suki quickly stuffed her books and papers onto her book bag. She felt the coolness of drool on her cheek and looked around to see if anyone was watching her. Everyone had left for the night. She self-consciously wiped her cheek with her sleeve. Pushing an almost empty water bottle and her phone into the bag, she threw the backpack on and headed towards the door. If she broke the curfew it would be reported to the university and might jeopardize her scholarship. She could never afford to pay the tuition herself should she fail.

The lights dimmed again, this time accompanied by chimes followed by the smarmy voice of the librarian. "The library is closing in fifteen minutes. The restrooms are closed."

Suki tried to rattle the restroom door handle, flagging down the janitor as he passed. "Can you open it for a moment? I really have to pee."

The janitor glanced towards the librarian and back at Suki, wagging his head. "Try the public restroom in the park."

Out on the steps of the library the warm, late August night wind blew, but did not cool her temper. She, Michiko and Kuno originally chose to study at the university library, rather than in their dorm room, to save on air conditioning costs.

Suki heard her phone vibrate in her book bag. It was still on silent mode from studying. Putting her bag on the ground, she squatted next to it, rummaging towards the source of the noise. She could not see under the dim light but felt her Kuromi phone charm and pulled it out. Michiko gave Kuromi to her saying Suki was cute like Hello Kitty, but with a vaguely dark side, like Kuromi's black jester hood sporting a pink skull.

"Hello?"

"Suki, where are you?" It was Michiko. "We just got back and you're not here."

"Sorry, I wanted to leave the library by eight, but fell asleep."

"It's late, take a taxi. I'll make us some udon when you get here."

Suki knew from her voice that Michiko had been drinking. "Are you sure? You know that you can't cook."

"What are you talking about? I can bake water just fine." Michiko laughed. "C'mon, get home soon, Kuno's rummaging around and there'll be no food left when you get here. Bye."

Suki smiled. "Bye." Having someone who cared about her felt nice. It took the edge off of her anger leaving only a mild annoyance behind.

Standing up, she pulled her wallet out of the bag and looked to see how much money she had, but Suki splurged on okonomiyaki for lunch and now there was not enough left for a taxi.

"It will be a week before I get my next stipend from the state scholarship board. I guess I'll have to walk…" She felt pressure on her bladder. "…Very quickly."

The six-block walk back to the dorm only took twenty minutes along well-lit streets and was uneventful… until Osaka Road.

Before nine – before office workers, tradesmen, and assorted losers started serious drinking – it was safe for students to travel down this road. But, after ten, after the alcohol had time to gestate and bring out dashed hopes and disappointments of men too impotent to change their sad little lives, the monsters oozed out onto Osaka Road.

Suki hesitated at the corner, standing under the last fully functioning streetlight, and watched the undulating shadows move along the street like evil black ants. The only illumination along the road was one dim and barely working, smashed streetlight, and the ambient glow of red neon from bars, strip joints, Image Clubs and Pink Salons that dotted the far side of the street. Loud music spilled out of clubs, washing the drunken effluent of humanity out onto the streets and into the gutters, where they smoked talked, laughed, shouted, argued, and fought. She saw ominous suggestions of drunken thugs, and lechers lingering around the clubs.

She steeled herself and said, "Come now, Suki, one last block and you're home." The thought of having to go down the same street she passed along without a concern this morning, now terrified her. It was only fifty meters to the corner where she was within a safe distance of her dorm. She waited for a time to see if a police patrol would come by. They usually drove by every half hour. Maybe they could escort her home. "Where are they? I have to go to a bathroom!" She said, as she fidgeted.

She decided to make a dash for it, walking briskly – not running – she figured that she could reach the far corner and the safety of her dorm before anyone noticed. The sounds of her footsteps were too loud, echoing off the brick walls of the boarding houses that fronted the road, so she tried to jog along quickly, tiptoeing to sneak by.

Her awkward movement caught a predator's eye. Like a pack of dogs, smelling fear and fresh meat, they followed her scent. Moving across the street behind her, following her, flipping her skirt they made rude propositions. One man, apparently their leader, cut her off. It was near the darkest part of the road with a parked truck blocking the view of the street. "Hey, sweet thing, wanna join us for a few drinks, and…"

Suki recoiled from his lewd suggestion, as well as the foul odor of stale smoke and liquor on his breath. She tried to squeeze along the wall past him.

"Hey, its rude to walk away while I'm talking." He pinned her arms against the wall, causing her to drop her bag. The truck hid their assault from prying eyes as she glanced around to see men on her left and right, cutting off any escape... and all hope.

Suki was cold and numb with fear. "I-I-I'll scream…!" Her protest was choked and weak.

"Then I'll just have to cut your throat to keep you quiet." He put a hand over her mouth.

Cheered on by his drunken buddies, the man put his other hand on Suki's bare thigh. He drew it up under her skirt as she tried to push it away. He groped clumsily at her panties. She clamped her legs together so he could not pull them off, but fear and hyperventilation made her lightheaded: She felt faint.

Her weakened condition caused her legs to release their grip, allowing him to tug her blue-stripped panties down to her knees. The man spun her around violently and mashed her up against the wall face first. He hiked her skirt up exposing her buttocks as his cronies hooted. Suki was losing consciousness as she ineffectively struggled. She was just too weak and knew she'd eventually have to give her body over to her assailants.

"No! Please stop… STOP!" She let out a scream with what little strength she had left.

Suki felt his clumsy, probing hand between her thighs. She wanted to fight back. Clamping her thighs and buttocks as tight as she could, she stopped his probing hand inside a trap of resolute flesh.

"You'd better cooperate with us and let me in, or else I'll stick something else hard – and sharp - into you!" The thug's hand was stuck between her legs.

Fear overtook her body; her limbs became cold from blood loss as her body prepared for his assault. Her body responded to this act of violence and terror in a most natural way. She felt a warm trickle travel down her legs to the pavement below.

"Damn, the bitch is peeing on me!"

Through the veil of fear, Suki, became aware of the sounds of the men: It had changed – the cheering ceased. She was not sure if it was because she grossed them out, or if she had just blocked out the sounds, but it had stopped. The pressure holding her to the wall eased and she fell to the ground. Before blacking out, she saw the thug who was about to sodomize her, fly off of her, backwards into the darkness.

Her last moments of consciousness were a jumble, but she had the hazy impression of a pale face, half hidden in the shadow of a hat… and a white mustache.

Warmth covered Suki's face like a pleasant masque; an intense light shone pink through closed eyelids. She cracked open her eyes, the light blinded her, if only for a brief moment and she saw blurry figures hovering above her. A spasm of panic began to swell in her breast until her eyes finally focused – the face of the dorm nurse stared down at her and a policewoman stood behind her. Suki turned her head on the pillow and looked beyond the lights. In the gap space between the curtains of the examination room, she saw Michiko sobbing on Kuno's shoulder.

"Wha.. wh…?" Suki panicked when she couldn't speak.

"Here is some water, dear." The doctor helped her to sit upright. "I'm nurse Ozawa and this is Officer Katame. We're here to help you Suki."

Suki took hold of the cup from the nurse's hand and drank. "Where am I?"

"In your dorm nurse's office. How are you feeling?"

She sat there quietly taking a mental inventory of her body, looking for wounds. "Aside from a small headache, I'm fine." Then Suki blushed. She looked under the covers and felt around her crotch. Her panties were there – and dry. She sighed with relief.

The nurse leaned forward and whispered. "Don't worry dear, after I made an examination to determine that you were not harmed, I cleaned you up." She looked behind her through the curtains. "Your roommate brought you fresh clothes and I dressed you."

Suki was relieved. "Thank you."

Michiko peeked in through the break in the curtain. "How are you Suki-chan?" Her eyes were puffy. "I'm so sorry for not being there. I should have been with you tonight, not singing karaoke!" She ran forward to the bed and they embraced. "Forgive me!"

The smell of alcohol was still on Michiko's breath. "The nurse says I'm okay. Nothing happened." Suki gave her a reassuring smile.

"Still, you were assaulted." Officer Katame held up a bag. "I'll need your clothes to examine for evidence."

"I-I am not comfortable having strangers looking over my wet undies." She blushed, and then nodded. "I guess it's okay."

The officer put the evidence in a box and then looked at Suki as she prepared to leave. "Do you have any questions before I go?"

"Just one."

"Yes?"

"How did I get here?"

The nurse looked as Suki. "The dorm mother said a white man carried you in here. Then he ran back out as quickly as he came in, telling her to call a doctor and the police. I guess he was going back to wrap up the brutes who attacked you."

The policewoman explained, "By the time we arrived around the corner, the assault suspect was unconscious, sitting under a lamppost waiting for us with his hands and feet tied by his own belt."

"I think I remember a face: and a white mustache."

Michiko gazed at Suki with a quizzical expression on her face. "Mr. Ted?"

"Mr. Ted? Who is that?" The nurse asked Michiko.

"He's an old white man we see working out in the courtyard below our dorm room early in the morning. The neighbors call him Ted-san. They say he's pleasant but he doesn't speak much."

Officer Katame looked to Suki, "Do you know a Gaikokujin, this 'Mr. Ted' person?"

Suki looked down at her hands, folded on the blanket before her. "No, I don't." She gazed up at Michiko.

Michiko furrowed her brow as she stared into Suki's face. "What's with that weird smile?"

Indebtedness

Suki had to be at the corner bakery early, at six o'clock, as soon as they opened. That was when the rice cakes were their freshest. If she wanted to get them to Mr. Ted in time Suki had to be at his gate before he slept. She certainly couldn't sleep after the shock of the previous night. Within minutes she found herself standing before his gate, gift in hand. She wanted to ring the bell but found her hand withdrawing. "What's to fear? After all, he saved me from the bad guys." She pulled the cord, the bell clanged and her heart leapt.

A small man with a globular face answered the gate. He looked down at her. "May I help you?"

"I have come to give this to Ted-san." Suki held up the rice cakes.

The initial look on his face was confusion, as if asking himself: 'why would a schoolgirl give a gift to an old man?' Suki realized that he was probably unaware of the incident outside his gate the night before. He shrugged with his eyes. "Oh, then you should come inside." He opened the gate and beckoned her to enter. "I am Hideo, the property superintendent. And you are…"

"Ona Suki." She whispered to Hideo, walking behind him and feeling more awkward with each step. "I don't want to disturb him. I just want to leave these for him."

"Not a problem, he just finished his daily exercise a moment ago and is probably cooling down with some tea." He looked over his shoulder and smiled at her. "After five years, you get to know someone's habits." He kicked off his shoes. "Wait here. I'll fetch him so you won't have to remove your shoes."

Suki watched as Hideo walked down towards Mr. Ted's room. She shifted her weight from one foot to the other, wondering if this as a good idea. If not a good idea, it was at least a social obligation to thank the hero who saved her chastity. The nobleman was due his reward.

Hideo approached with Mr. Ted behind, still dressed in his workout clothes and sporting a towel around his neck.

What struck Suki was Mr. Ted's height. Though still above her on the wooden deck, he stood a good head and a half over Hideo, who was a bit taller than her. He was at least 182 centimeters, or more and the dogi he wore hung from broad shoulders.

The pale face peering down at her was of a man into his fifties or early sixties, but not old and wrinkled as she thought it might be. Telling age in Caucasians was, at best, difficult. Some lines around intense, squinting blue eyes and wide, firm mouth belied a face that at one time laughed, but had now ceased. It was a good face for a good man.

Sporting a full head of hair there was gray among dark brown patches. Above his lip was the white mustache she saw the night before. She was so enamored by his appearance that she almost forgot her reason for coming. Then she realized that he might not know Japanese and spoke in English. "I want to thank you for what you did for me."

He stepped down from the deck, stopped and stood before her.

Suki bowed and hastily pushed the package towards him. "Good Morning! I wish to express great thanks and indebtedness to you. Please accept this humble gift as a token of my gratitude!" She was afraid her English was not as good as his and was self conscious about what she had said. However, she continued bowing, eyes down, as she held out the cakes.

The package was lightly lifted from her hands. Gazing up, she saw the top of his head in a respectful bow, in keeping with their respective ages. He accepted her gift with both hands.

"Domo Arigato, Miss…"

"I am Suki, Ona Suki." She righted herself and gave him a relieved smile.   "I didn't know you spoke Japanese."

He answered in Nippongo.   "I am happy to hear your perfect English as well."

She backed away. "I must go to class now. Goodbye!"

Walking to the gate, she stopped and turned. "Thank you for your help in saving my dignity from those men last night. You are a hero to me!" She quickly bowed again out of respect.

He waved back to her, smiled, and held her gift as she left through the gate.

Walking from the third floor stairwell towards her English class, she heard Miss Kusawa called to her from behind.

"Suki, do you have a moment?

"Yes, Miss Kusawa. How may I help you?"

Approaching Suki, Miss Kusawa held out an index card. "I thought of you when I saw this on the board in the teacher's lounge this morning."

Suki read it.   'Intern needed to help edit an English language blog on Japanese linguistics. Apply at 49 Osaka Road.' Suki looked at Miss Kusawa with a blank stare.

Miss Kusawa pointed to the card. "It'll help expand your knowledge of English. Why don't you go there and see if it's for you?"

"Thank you Miss Kusawa. It's near where I live so I will go there this afternoon."

Walking down along Osaka road she passed the spot of her attack, a return of the previous night's fear washed over her. Suki felt a hard pit in her stomach and could still feel a hand and her pee on her legs. It was humiliating. Moving quickly past the spot, she buried her nose in the card with the address on it. "41 Osaka Road, 45…47…" Looking up she saw number 49. She stopped, staring at the gate and the house beyond. "Oh, my…"

It was Mr. Ted's house.

"Oh, Miss I am so happy to see you! And to know you are well." Hideo let her in. "After you left this morning my neighbor told me all about your ordeal and how Mr. Ted came to your rescue."

Suki showed him the card. "Is this the right address, Hideo-san? Am I to see someone here about a job?"

He looked at the card and smiled. "Yes, it is here. Let me take you to him." He closed the gate behind her. "Oh the news of your rescue made Mr. Ted a neighborhood celebrity. He is a humble and private man, so when the neighborhood women approached him in the market today to thank him for saving a young girl from some perverts, he became… uncomfortable."

"I'm sorry if I caused him any problems."

"Oh, on the contrary, when you gave him those rice cakes, he had a big smile as he shared some with me. I have not seen such a smile on his face since he moved in here four years ago. He said it was like his Miko's sweets."

"Who's Miko?"

Hideo turned solemn. "It's heartbreaking, really. Miko

was his wife. She died suddenly and tragically. I do not know the details, only that he still mourns her and prays at her shrine everyday." He looked over his shoulder at her. "In any case your gift brought him much happiness, so I thank you."

She felt a little blush pass across her face. "You are welcome."

He brought her to the door of Mr. Ted's room and knocked lightly. After a moment and some rustling inside, he came and opened it. He was still as big as Suki remembered, even though he stood on a step in their last meeting.

Mr. Ted wore a non-descript white shirt and black slacks. "Hideo-san, how may I help you?"

Suki found Mr. Ted's Japanese to be flawless.

Hideo handed the card to Mr. Ted. "This young lady wishes to be your intern."

Mr. Ted looked at Suki. "You are the girl who gave me the sweets this morning." He did not mention the attack, and that gave her great relief. "How are you?"

"I am well, thank you." Suki gave a bow. "I hope you enjoyed them."

"Very much, thank you."

"I am Ona Suki, a fourth year student at the University majoring in English studies." She gave a respectful bow to him as he was her senior and about to become her Sensei. "I would be honored to become your intern."

"Come in Miss Ona, and leave the door open please."

Suki entered the room. It was mostly books and papers surrounding a desk with a notebook computer on it. Around the corner was the living space separated by a shoji screen. She peered around the place as Mr. Ted went to the kitchen. Still speaking in Japanese, he called out to her. "Water, juice or tea?"

"Pardon me?"

He peeked his head from around the corner. "Would you like water, juice or tea to drink?"

"Oh, water will be fine."

He returned with two bottles of water on a tray and offered her one.

Suki spoke in English. "Would you be more comfortable speaking in English? That is why I came here… to learn."

Mr. Ted nodded.

Nervously sitting in silence, Suki saw numerous volumes of books. Some were in English but most were Japanese. There were other languages as well, Chinese, Tagalog and Vietnamese. She spotted the name Edward Langdon Therioux on a few volumes over his desk. "Oh, that is English professor's favorite author." She produced her own volume of Pacific Paradox from her bag.

Mr. Ted leaned forward. "May I see it?"

Suki noticed his large arms. He seemed very powerful. Though she didn't recall it, others told of how he pummeled her attacker with two blows and ran carrying her to the dorm doctor. She thought that he must be very fit to have done that. But then, she had watched him work out from her balcony overlooking his courtyard almost every day for a month. He did not seem as old as she originally thought. She gave a brief smile as she handed the book to him.

Taking the book, he flipped through the pages. "This is an older edition written for the North American market." He paused and looked back over his shoulder to the wall of books behind him. Taking down a volume he inspected it and handed it to Suki. "This is the latest edition for the Japanese market. It's written in parallel passages of English and Nippongo for comparative study. Also the footnotes explain many more current cultural idioms and sayings. I think you will find this more helpful."

She leafed through it and beamed. "This is much better. I will show it to my English professor." She looked at Mr. Ted. "I cannot take your copy. It would not be right."

"Please, take it. I can always get another. Consider it a gift on your first day of work."

He explained her duties to come in twice a week and update the blog and to answer emails. That would free him up to write a new book. At the end of their meeting he escorted her to the door of the compound and bade her goodbye.

"Thank you Mr. Ted."

"We're going to be working together so just call me Ted."

"Yes, Ted-san."

At her bow, he grinned for the first time. Though he was

not required to, he returned her bow out of approval. She found him to be very polite and proper, not at all how she pictured Americans to be.

Turning to leave, the memorial to Miko caught her attention. The woman in the picture was smiling, but for a brief moment, she thought she saw a scowl cross the face in the picture. Suki guessed it was a trick of lighting.

The next morning Suki was on her balcony perch watching Ted work out in the garden below, comfortable in the knowledge she would become his assistant and possibly a friend... or... perhaps, something more?

To Love a Gaijin

After English class Suki stayed behind, standing in the shadows until everyone left. She crept towards Miss Kusawa's desk so quietly that it startled her teacher.

"Oh, Suki! I didn't see you there." She collected herself with a smile for her prized student. "What is it, dear?"

She held out the book. "I wanted to show you this volume of Pacific Paradox. It's new."

"Hmmm. I didn't know he brought out a new edition." She looked it over and leafed through the pages with a frown. "Too bad it took a foreigner to write something like this, but it is a western observation of Japanese idioms and culture. Still, his work is well done. I think I'll incorporate this into next semester's curriculum." She handed the volume back to Suki "Only until I find a better textbook by a Japanese author." Miss Kusawa's face brightened, "By the way, how did that lead pan out for you?"

Suki was confused. "Lead?"

"The internship? The card I gave you yesterday?"

"Oh, it..." She began to answer but after her reaction to the book's author Suki thought she should keep it to herself. "I'm giving it serious consideration."

"Good. Let's talk over something sweet to eat. My blood sugar drops like a stone this time of day."

Miss Kusawa led Suki across the quad and out to the street until they found the local ice cream shop.

"What do you say we talk over parfaits?"

Suki smiled at her teacher's suggestion. It was as though she was being invited to be her friend, to have girl talk. Suki first experienced that sensation with Michiko. "That would be nice."

They sat down and looked at the menu. "I'll have a chocolate parfait. How about you Suki?"

Suki scoured the menu for the cheapest thing she could find.

She felt Miss Kusawa's hand on hers.

"It's my treat, so splurge!"

"I never had a parfait, what would you recommend?"

"Well I'm partial to chocolate, but there's caramel and strawberry too."

"Can I try strawberry?"

"Sure you can!" When the waitress came, she ordered for the both of them.

"What kind of ice cream do you usually like?"

Suki looked at her teacher. "Well once, Michiko bought me an ice cream cone. It was vanilla. So, I guess I like vanilla."

"Is that the flavor your parents bought you when you were a little girl?"

Suki broke eye contact with Miss Kusawa and looked down. "They never bought me ice cream."

Miss Kusawa gazed at the girl. "Oh. That's… a pity."

Suki picked up her water. "Did your mother and father buy you ice cream?"

"Well, yes, of course they did. Many times."

"Were they nice to you? I mean which one did you like best, your mother or your father?"

Before the teacher could answer, the waitress brought the parfaits to the women and placed them on the table. Suki's eyes grew large looking at the ice cream cup. "Wow, this is awesome!" She looked over at her sensei, almost asking permission to eat it.

Miss Kusawa was amused and smiled. "Well, it's not going to eat itself. Dig in!"

After a few moments of eating in silence, Suki looked over at her teacher. "Which one was white?"

Miss Kusawa looked at her, perplexed.

"Your mother or your father? Which one was the white one?" She asked it so directly that it caught Miss Kusawa off guard.

"Well, it was my father…"

"Is he American?"

"No. He's Canadian."

"Is he nice to your mother?"

"Well, she's dead…"

"Oh, it must have been very hard on him!"

Miss Kusawa was flustered by her questions. "I-I don't recall… we grew apart many years ago. We haven't spoken since her death."

Suki knew she was hitting a raw nerve with her professor. "I'm sorry, I just wanted to know more about how foreign men see Japanese women."

"How does any man see any woman? If you look beyond the façade and into the person, then should it matter?" We see one another through the filter of mutual need. Staring into her parfait while picking at it, Miss Kusawa was quiet.

"That's not as important as how Japanese men view Japanese women who love foreign men… or worse, Japanese men who love foreign women." Miss Kusawa toyed with the remaining ice cream in her cup.

"Suki, do you really want to know what it is like to love a gaijin?"

Suki was quiet and didn't answer. She felt shamed for embarrassing her sensei.

"My father adored my mother. He, being a stranger and alien to this land, had no one but her to turn to, few men accept a foreigner taking *their* women. Her family, friends and neighbors disowned her for marrying a gaijin. Only their love for each other carried them along with two half-breed children – a girl and boy. We lived on an island of love – all by ourselves."

"That must have been hard on you and your brother."

"When you are the product of two races, there is a struggle that comes to you whether you like it or not: You have to reject one half of you. Kenji and I took different paths of rejection.

"We were both bullied at school for being different. When you are bullied, you either fight, or you submit. I submitted and Kenji fought.

"I submitted to the will of bullies and embraced my Japanese side. I worked hard to be one of them. Because I looked different I could never be accepted, but I tried to fit in; speaking better; acting better than they did; to prove my loyalty – to prove myself to them – and to myself.

"By the time Kenji he got to high school, he was tough and would fight almost every day. He joined with other white, Gaikokujin boys and formed a gang that was always getting into trouble. He rejected the Japanese half of his heritage when they rejected him.

"Kenji also rejected me because I immersed myself in all things Japanese but still always found myself on the outside. Friends would not come to my house when I invited them. I was not invited to go with them for fear their families would be scandalized." She smiled anemically and winked at Suki. "It was especially so if my friends had brothers who might become enamored by the exotic foreign chick."

"Yes, I watch how boys follow you with their eyes. You are very beautiful and very..." She let her eyes wander to Miss Kusawa's breasts.

Miss Kusawa followed Suki's eyes and grinned. "...Stacked? That's the Canadian side. Well it does get the boy's attention in class so I know they're looking at me and not out the window."

"Isn't that a rude term in English?"

"Yes, but I've heard far ruder terms about my body and what the boys wanted to do with it."

Suki suddenly thought of Kuno. "Uh, yeah. I've heard that too... So, is there a man who likes you?"

"Dozens!"

"Are there any that you like?"

"None."

For a moment neither woman said anything.

"Well, there was one boy, once, a while ago.

"We became very close at the university. A university is like a cloister that shields you from the outside world – the real world beyond. He fell for me and I adored him. He made the terrible mistake of bringing me home with him. You see, he came from a prominent political family and was being groomed for public service by his father. Once they saw me with him, his father berated him in front of me and even referred to me as a whore as I stood there. His mother suggested that he could keep me as a mistress after he was properly married."

"That is so horrendous! What did the boy do?"

"Nothing."

"Nothing?"

"Nothing. He just took it. So not to further shame him, I stood there and took it too. He loved me, but his family was right; having me as a wife would have kill his career."

Miss Kusawa looked out the window and recalled the humiliating episode dispassionately, but the reflection in the glass betrayed a glistening teardrop running down her cheek.

"I am allowed to be an exotic object of men's fantasies, not a real woman. 'Yet, the allure of an object fades once it is possessed; but to enjoy a woman's genuine love delights a man into his old age'."

Suki found her own eyes getting dewy.

"That is what it is to love a gaijin."

Inflection

Over the following weeks Suki found working with Ted to be a learning experience and often an exercise in patience. In writing mode, when he had to be the most creative with his subject, interrupting him could bring on a wicked glare. In editing mode, when he was revising the text, he could be quite talkative.   One afternoon, tending to his editing, he looked over at Suki. "How is your grasp of English coming along? Is the site helping you to understand more about the cultural distinctions between different English-speaking nationalities?"

"Some, but I have a difficult time understanding if the writer is serious, sarcastic, happy or angry."

"Unlike the spoken word where we use voice inflection to add a third dimension of meaning, written language - which is more two dimensional - takes greater skill to convey mood. It is sometimes better to read a phrase in context to the whole of the message. That's what semantics is all about."

"Miss Kusawa said the same thing; that English is a fluid

language that to flow as it must, it adapts to changes, not unlike the way a creek flows around a rock placed in its path. Japanese is far older but with many more subtle combinations in a very traditional, nuanced visual pattern of communication."

Ted was quiet for a long moment. "Would that be Kusawa Ayako?" His voice was pensive, low and his tone puzzled Suki.

"Yes, she is my English professor. Do you know her?"

"By reputation." He turned his face back to his computer screen. "I heard her speak last year in Manila, at an ASEAN conference on education. She gave a lecture about the cultural blending of foreign and indigenous languages within homogeneous societies. She saw it as a form of an emerging subculture identity that united minorities, giving them a form of code communications to protect them from persecution: Like American slang of jazz musician's in the 1920's. I found her to be very… impressive."

"She's really pretty too."

He turned towards her with a crooked smile. "Yeah, that part was hard to miss." He returned to his editing.

Suki wondered if Ted would like Miss Kusawa. After talking to her that morning, Suki reckoned that Miss Kusawa would not like Ted because of what he was: a thought that made Suki oddly happy.

In the early dawn as the girls rested on their dorm room balcony Michiko nestled her chin on her hands along the railing and glanced over at Suki. "So what are you going to do about him?" She gestured with a nod of her head to the courtyard below.

Across the balcony Suki mirrored Michiko's pose. "What can I do?" The daily viewing of Ted's workout had become a regular form of entertainment for the girls. Now that she was closer to him, she had a chance to appreciate his best and worst qualities. "I guess I'll just sit here getting hot and frustrated." Sometimes Suki indulged in fantasies about the two of them together. She peered at Michiko. "We're falling into a rut."

"Us or you and him?"

"Both."

"Must be tough working with the guy, feeling the way you do about him." Michiko said.

"I try to concentrate on my work and not stare at him. That's not easy"

"Does he ever look at you?"

"Yes, when we're discussing something."

"No, you know what I mean; does he ever try to sneak a peek up your skirt or down your blouse?"

Suki laughed. "Michiko, you have a fertile, yet twisted and perverted, imagination!"

"It's no surprise the way you dress."

Suki creased her brow and glared over at Michiko. "What's that supposed to mean?"

"You dress like a schoolteacher! You need to get a flip skirt, frilly low cut blouse and a pushup bra if you want to get his attention. Then let your skirt accidently hike up when bending over and sit with your legs subtly parted while wearing frilly panties, a thong, or better yet, nothing at all! Suki-chan, if you want him, you have to seduce him!"

Suki looked and Michiko and gave a nervous chortle. "Hee-hee, what makes you think I want to seduce him?"

"Stand up!" Michiko demanded.

"What?"

"Stand up and turn around!"

Suki complied, standing and turning around as ordered. On the back of her nightgown was a wet spot.

"I rest my case."

"I am such a pervert!" She sat back down and buried her head in her arms. "Being a secretor, I can't even hide it! It's so hard being a voyeur."

"Speaking of hard, do you think he still can?"

Michiko's question confused Suki. "'Can' what?"

Michiko made a circle with her finger and thumb and poked another finger through it, moving it rapidly back and forth.

"Oh my!" Suki's cheeks turned bright red and she put her hand to her mouth. "I never thought about that!"

"He is kind of old. Maybe he's…" Michiko let her finger

go limp.

"Hideo-san said his wife died some years ago." Suki earnestly asked Michiko, "Do you think he's had a woman since then?"

Michiko was looking down at Ted as she answered. "Oh, I'm sure he's had a woman."

Her quick answer annoyed Suki. "How can you be so sure, Michiko! You don't know that!" Suki became irritated and sounded jealous. "You can't know that!"

Michiko turned back to Suki, pointing in Ted's direction.

Suki looked over the edge of the balcony and down at Ted. He had stopped and was talking to someone emerging from behind the trees of the yard. She saw a woman with long, wet, black hair from behind, and she was wearing a bathrobe. She brought tea out to him and kissed his cheek as she handed him the cup. After a few moments of talking, they walked back behind the trees together.

"One mystery solved." Michiko extended her finger stiffly upward. "And another one begins: Who is that mystery woman?"

Suki sullenly stood up and went inside to change.

Killer

Others often saw Suki as strange and moody, but throughout that day, her soul emitted a depressing darkness, which crept through her skin, threatening to infect others with a dire pathogen.

It carried over into the afternoon, into her work time with Ted. She pecked lifelessly away at the emails that asked for advice and information about trans cultural linguistics; the topic of the month on the Edward Langdon Therioux's, Paradoxically Speaking, blog site. The vision of the other woman, her black hair wet from a bath and wearing Ted's bathrobe seared into Suki's brain and wouldn't release its grip. The woman's kiss played like an endless loop all day long.

"Suki?"

The voice was deep and disembodied as the computer screen hypnotized her and probed at her brain for answers.

"Suki? Are you all right?" It came back into her thoughts and she blinked, realizing it was not a daydream. She bolted upright, startled. Ted was looking over his shoulder at her. "You've been kind of droopy since you arrived. Not the usual perky Suki."

She stared blankly at Ted. In Suki's imagination, The Evil One from this morning was there, sneaking yet another kiss of his cheek as Suki looked at his face.

"Oh, no. I am okay. Its just that…"

Ted had stopped typing and looked at her.

"I'm…" She desperately wanted to ask him about the other woman. It gnawed at her chest to keep it in. "How is it said in America? 'On the rag'?" It was a lie, but she needed an excuse.

"Oooh, yeah, that's a rough time." Ted grimaced. "Different women; different reactions. Say, you're not one of those PMS man killers, are you?" He gave Suki a furtive smile.

Suki found herself laughing quietly despite her cross mood. "No. It just cramps and makes me fatigued." The smile broke her out of her mood.

"I know its rough on a woman. You can go home if you want to."

She demurred with a child's smile. "I'll be fine if I can lay flat for a few minutes. "

"Sure, there's a small futon for guests against the far wall. Feel free to use it anytime you need to."

She walked through the dim room, over near the wall. Clearing a pile of books, she laid the mat out on the floor and lay in a position where she could see the room. Ted smiled and went back to his editing to give her some privacy. The mat was on the floor next to the memorial shrine to his late wife. Suki stared at her picture with the black ribbons draped diagonally at the top of the silver frame. The traditional bowl of rice was offered and he had recently burned incense to her memory. Its patchouli aroma lingered in the room like a whorehouse madam's stale sulfuric ghost. Yet Suki could also detect the sweet aroma of a woman's herbal shampoo beneath the staleness. Miko's picture was not a formal one, but rather one a lover might snap while on an outing. The sun from behind gave her hair an aura, a halo, like a saint. Her face beamed a radiant smile and there was a slightly naughty twinkle in her eye. She loved the photographer.

"She's so beautiful." Suki was unaware she had spoken aloud.

"What was that?" Ted glanced across the room at the picture.

"I didn't mean to disturb you. I'm sorry. Its just that I find your wife to be quite beautiful."

For a moment, all in the room was still. The flies that often annoyed her on the late summer days and landed on her computer monitor – forming moving punctuation – were absent, hiding in anticipation of the next moments. Even the dust caught in the sunbeams seemed to hover, waiting. Ted twisted his chair to face the shrine and Suki resting on the floor behind it.

He leaned back and interlaced his hands on his lap in

contemplation. "That is my favorite picture of her because it most reminds me of what she was like in life. Miko was my wife and my lover and my best friend: the womanly trinity in its perfection. I breathed her in every morning and exhaled her each evening. We had few friends, but we had each other: that was enough."

"You still love her."

"We were married twenty five years." He looked in the direction of the picture. "My life began and ended with her."

Suki almost cried at the love he had for his dead wife. She should cry for herself as well: could she ever know a love like this from any man?

She gazed at Miko's picture wanting to imagine what their life together might have been like. Yet, a taboo question lingered in the air like the piercing sunbeam in the dark room: How did she die? Was it cancer? Was it an accident... suicide?

"What happened?" Before Suki realized it, she asked a very personal question, the socially forbidden one that might cause him pain, and her humiliation. "No-no, please! It is none of my business! I'm sorry!"

Ted's face did not change expression as he turned in his seat and faced his computer monitor.

Suki had offended him.

A sullen silence covered the room as Suki pretended to be resting to cover her mortification. The picture of the pretty woman who stared out at her became something new to her: a model for the type of woman Ted loved, and still, a possible rival for his affections. It was hard to be jealous of a dead woman, but Suki was sure that she would be compared to Miko if she and Ted should ever…

Her thoughts and the silence of the room gave away to Ted's voice.

"I-I…" He stayed hunched over his computer as he haltingly spoke to her.

Suki saw him take a deep breath and let it out. "To answer your question…" He was barely audible, but she heard him clearly in the hushed room.

"I killed her."

Was it Suki's imagination or did a chilling wind wash over her on that late summer day?

Stalking and Conspiracy

Michiko's eyes widened and Kuno's jaw went slack.

"Why didn't you run out of the room screaming?" Kuno laughed in tense disbelief. The crowd of students moving along the corridor dampened his tone of panic.

Michiko echoed Kuno's bewilderment. "The man confesses that he killed his pretty young wife and, tell us again what you did?"

Suki said quietly, "I got up, went over to my terminal and continued my work. When I had finished, I said goodnight to him and that I would see him on Thursday."

"Are you mad?" This time, Michiko's bellow drew stares and a few gasps. She leaned over to Suki and whispered through gritted teeth, "You're going to go back to work for a confessed murderer?" Her anger made Suki blush.

Suki bent her head down, looking at her feet. "It's not like that. If you saw the picture of his wife, you would have known that there was a deep and lingering love in her eyes. His daily prayers and offerings tell me that he still deeply loves and mourns her. Ted's not the kind of man who could rise to the level of anger needed to murder anyone." She raised her head back up in defiance. "No, I think that he must have meant it another way.

Kuno asked, "How did she die?"

Suki stared at Kuno. "What?"

He repeated the question. "How did his wife die?"

Suki's answer was barely audible in the din of the hallway. "He-he didn't say."

Michiko placed her arm around her friends shoulder to comfort her. "Well that's what the Internet's for, isn't it?"

In the library the three of them crowded around the glaring monitor. Kuno sat in the chair and Michiko leaned on his one shoulder and Suki the other, which by his expression pleased him.

A fellow student passed by and called to Kuno, "What's you secret with the ladies, Kuno?"

"Charisma! And a really huge p…" Kuno turned his head to answer his friend and saw Michiko making a pinching motion with her nails. "Personality!"

"Oooh, Good save!" Michiko smiled at him. "What did you find?"

"I searched the databases for obituaries from around the country and found nothing despite the unusual surname."

"She may have been listed under her maiden name. Some papers, especially in the provinces only use Japanese names since foreign names don't translate well into Kanji. Did you try the police reports?"

"Not yet." Kuno logged onto the national police register website and typed in Therioux+death. Within a minute, and after scrolling down, there was a brief news story from Agata, a northern village in Akita Prefecture. "Here's something!"

Six eyes scoured the record of an accident report that was taken by an officer on a remote mountain highway. Kuno read it aloud. "A foreigner named Edward Therioux had swerved on an icy road and skidded broadside into a lamppost. The car caught on fire and he was burned trying to pull his wife out of the car. The report said he had been drinking and was taken to the local hospital for treatment of second and third degree burns. Charges were filed and he was incarcerated for drunk driving and involuntary manslaughter."

Michiko looked at the profile of Suki's face lit by the monitor, her eyes transfixed on the screen. "It's not much, but it says it all."

Kuno said, "At least we now know that he didn't murder her."

"He did." Suki couldn't take her eyes off of the screen. "In his mind, he murdered her."

Michiko watched Suki stand upright. "Hey, the guy isn't bad, you said it yourself: he couldn't purposely kill anyone. Remember, he saved you from being raped and possibly even maimed or murdered. He's really a good guy!"

Kuno offered, "Maybe he's trying to atone for his past sins against her. He's trying to save others, like you from those pervs."

"You are right. He's trying to save his wife from the burning car all over again!" Suki looked at Michiko and Kuno. "Oh, how he must have suffered!" Suki began to weep. "That's why he doesn't talk to people; the heaviness in his heart makes him sad." She fell onto Kuno's shoulder and cried.

Kuno patted her on the shoulder. "Wow, Suki, you really have a crush on the old guy, don't you."

Michiko pinched Kuno on the arm.

"Ow! That hurts ya know!" He glared at Michiko as he continued to comfort Suki. "Well he is old enough to be her father, maybe even her grandfather." He asked Suki, "How old are you Suki?"

She raised her eyes from his shoulder. "Twenty."

"How old it Mr. Ted?" Michiko asked.

Suki was quiet and just blinked. "I-I don't know how old he is."

Kuno continued, "Did he ever tell you how old he was?"

Suki was looking up at him and over to Michiko with wet eyes. She sniffed. "No."

Kuno answered her. "I'll tell you… He's ancient, a graybeard, maybe sixty or seventy? Eighty?" He turned to Suki. "What do they call that kind of relationship in the in the west? Oh yeah, a May-December romance!"

"Well if he is eighty, he's the hottest eighty year old I've ever seen." Michiko face became flushed as she made a fanning motion.

"What do you mean?" Kuno eyed Michiko suspiciously.

Michiko's flush became a blush. "Well, you see, our balcony sort of overlooks his yard where he works out at his martial arts at dawn every day."

"You spy on Mr. Ted!?!"

That drew some stares from around the library and embarrassed Michiko.

"No!" She seethed. "We merely observe him."

Kuno leveled a glare at her. "How long have you 'observed' him?"

"Oh, let's see…" Michiko did some mental calculations with the aim of delaying her answer.

Suki piped in. "About two months."

Michiko gave her an annoyed stare.

"I take it back; you're not spying: You're stalking!"

Kuno turned his attention to Suki. "Suki-chan, You have to find out how old he is. It's important that you know."

"It is?"

"Of course!" Michiko took her hand. "You have to find out if he's still vital enough to handle a woman as young and alluring as yourself!"

"I do?"

"Speaking of the alluring part...""How can you ever seduce a man dressed like a bank teller? You're a bland person, aren't you?"

"Am I?"

Michiko became excited and pulled on Kuno's sleeve. "Maybe we can go shopping and I can give her some dressing tips!"

Suki's eyes lit up. "You can?"

"I don't know Michiko; I can't see her wearing your cosplay emo look.   Suki needs something more conservative, mature, and hot."

Michiko looked at Kuno, realizing they had the same idea. They smacked their fists to their palms at the same time as both said, "Miss Kusawa!"

Half sitting on the front edge of her desk, Miss Kusawa, eyed the three nervous students sitting in the front row desks. Her suspicious eyes darted back and forth between them. The class had gone, the doors were closed and the floor was devoid of students.

"Okay which of you is the ringleader?" Her eyes naturally set upon Kuno. "Let me get this straight. Suki needs a makeover to impress some boy, and you feel that – for some unknown reason – I would be the best fashion consultant for her? Is that about it?"

The three looked at her and then to each other and nodded their heads.

Kuno grinned at her. "You dress very conservatively but you wear your blouse low enough and your skirt high enough to tease. Plus your big green eyes, pouty lips and button nose with those cute freckles on it make you look like a doll. When you pass down the aisles, the guys shudder at your aroma. In short, Miss Kusawa…" He stood and pointed at her with an accusing finger. "You have been voted this university's hottest teacher by the male students and staff!"

The girls on either side of him were speechless and stared at him for making such a bold statement. Michiko was shocked by his forceful gesture. Looking at Miss Kusawa, they were not the only ones. Their teacher sat there, wide eyed and blushing. She soon shook off the initial shock. Narrowed her gaze at her accuser and stood to her full height of at least 182 centimeters in her heels.

Michiko and Suki watched as Miss Kusawa rose from her desk and moved slowly, menacingly towards Kuno. He was trying to back off, and fell back into his seat trapped in the desk's tight grip. She approached with a slow deliberation, as though she was thinking of a tough test question to ask him. She put on the glasses she had been holding as she twirled a pencil between her fingers.

"So, Kuno, you say that the boys think I'm hot?"

"Y-yes, Sensei, very much so."

Michiko snickered at Kuno's sudden formality.

Stopping about half a meter away from him, she reached down, pinched the seams of her skirt, hiked it up a bit. "Do you think they would like it if I wore my skirt this high?"

"Yes!"

She hiked it higher. "What about this high?"

All Kuno could do was stare, gulp and croak out a "Mmmm!"

Michiko and Suki couldn't contain their giggles at Kuno's predicament.

Moving her hips around with a fluid gyration, she turned around and, like a practiced stripper, slightly poked her butt towards him. "Or, maybe, this high?" She had pulled it up exposing the top seams of her pantyhose legs and giving just a suggestion of pantyless cheeks peeking out.

Then she made a three quarter turn back towards him and fiddled with her top blouse button. As he watched, she popped it open and her cleavage spread out a bit as more of it was now liberated.

"Should my top be this low, Kuno?"

Kuno was a deer in the headlights of the oncoming truck that was his teacher. He mindlessly followed her fingers wherever they went.

"Maybe…" She popped open another button. "This low?" Her breast quivered at the release and the rims of her lacey black bra began to peek out.

She reached behind her head and pulled the pins from the bun in hair, which she always wore up. She let it cascade down over her shoulders and breasts, shaking it free as it fell.

"Wow!" It was much longer than Michiko had ever

guessed, coming down to her waist. "You hair is gorgeous!"

She took off her glasses and seductively bit the stem, Kuno's eyes followed her every move.

She licked her lips and set them into a pout.

She closed the final gap between her and Kuno, standing to her full height, a cliff of breasts and a cascade of shiny blue-black hair towering over him.

He began to shake.

She placed her hands on the sides of the desk and leaned forward, giving Kuno a view of two plump white orbs straining against a one-size-too-small bra that bridged them with a single clip. "Is this what the boys want, Kuno, a naughty teacher?"

"Y-y-y… y-y…" He could not speak or take his eyes off her breasts. He had become an inhuman jellyfish.

"You know, Kuno," She place her hand gently under his chin and moved his eyes up to her face. "If you weren't so good for my ego," She puckered her lips and drew them closer to him. "I'd smack you good!"

"S-s-spa… spank me!" Kuno whimpered.

Miss Kusawa gave him a smile and then turned to Suki. "Is this the effect you want to have on your man, Suki?"

She looked at her teacher with bright eager eyes and grinned. "Yes, please!"

Corruptible Innocence

A man's hell on earth is summarized in one word: Shopping.

Kuno was paying for his sins with the worst form of contrition a man can endure, by joining the girls on their Let's-makeover-Suki trip. He gallantly offered to stay behind but Michiko took one hand and Miss Kusawa took the other. Trapped in their web he could not shake loose. Miss Kusawa said they needed to test the new look out on a susceptible male. Kuno was their chosen victim.

The first stop was for new makeup and hair. They took her to finally settling on highlights and red streaks rather than the completely blond cosplay look. For her makeup a copper lining with some bronze eye shadow and proper mascara to make her eyes bigger. Kuno suggested anime eyes, but they overruled him. A smoothing foundation and some color to the face and cheeks. Lipstick made her small mouth more pouting, and conservatively seductive.

Kuno's marathon misery was not yet over. Next: the clothes-shopping event. The girls went through racks like a typhoon, testing anything and everything on Suki.

"What does a man like a woman to wear?" Michiko asked Miss Kusawa.

Miss Kusawa whispered so Kuno would not hear. "Perfume and little else."

Michiko and Suki giggled.

"So, Suki, tell me more about this man of yours?"

"Well… he's a graduate… somewhat bookish and aloof… " Suki tried to describe Ted without giving away too much. She knew Miss Kusawa would not approve. "He barely notices me when I'm around… And he's physical."

Her last statement got a raised eyebrow from Miss Kusawa and a snicker from Michiko and Kuno.

"Okay." Miss Kusawa looked at Michiko and Kuno and back at Suki. "When you say he's physical, you mean…?" She drew out the last word in an effort to have Suki fill in the blank.

Suki paused.

Michiko stood next to Miss Kusawa, making the same gesture with her fingers that she made on the balcony just to tease her.

"Please, Michiko, that's rude!" Then she asked Suki, "Do you mean physical, like that?" She pointed at Michiko's hands.

Suki blushed, waving her hands as if wiping the thought off the board. "Oh, no, I mean that he likes to exercise and is very athletic."

"Oh well, he sounds perfectly respectable… and a bit boring. I think we need to take this attack in stages. Starting with a soft sell and ending with the nuclear option!"

Kuno leaned over and whispered to Michiko. "I think Miss Kusawa is getting into this a little too much. Suki doesn't want her to know that Ted is the target of her affections because she wouldn't approve, but if she keeps asking questions Suki might let it slip."

Michiko leaned over to Miss Kusawa. "The guy doesn't know about her feelings yet. She needs to have her actions tell him so he will make the first move."

"Ah-ha, a covert operation! I see. Well let's start by getting her out of those old clothes."

"What's wrong with my clothes?" Suki asked her.

Michiko answered her, "Nothing, if you want to be a virgin all your life. You dress as if you are your own mother. It says lifelong matron all over."

The girls accompanied Suki into the changing room. About five minutes later Miss Kusawa came out, found Kuno trying to escape and plopped him into a chair near the dressing room opening for a fashion show. Suki came out modeling the first dress. It was one that Suki chose and Kuno responded to it indifferently as Miss Kusawa watched him intently.

"Nope! Doesn't get a rise. Try the one Michiko chose."

After a few minutes, she came out again, this time displaying far more skin and a visible blush. Kuno's eyes widened. "Wow, is that Suki-chan?"

Miss Kusawa studied his expression. "Hmmm, better put that one into the nuclear arsenal."

The next outfit was a thin blouse with a low cut front and a flip skirt with frilly pink panties that showed when she bent over.

"Hey, that's quite a cleavage she developed there. How'd you get tits onto Suki?"

Suki got a cross look on her face. "Hey Kuno! I have tits, I just never showed them to you!"

Miss Kusawa shrugged. "Industrial strength push-up bra."

Kuno stroked his chin. "We're looking for flirty, but not skanky. The bra tries too hard. Better to go braless. Anyway her real tits are perky enough."

Miss Kusawa looked at him and smiled. "Good observation Kuno! Okay, Suki, lose the bra and lets have another look."

"With Kuno-sempai sitting there watching me? No way!"

"He's our surrogate boyfriend and besides I think he's right. Off with the jug hammocks."

She went in and came back out without the bra. Kuno stood up and walked over to her, circling slowly around her. She looked nervous and she started to tremble. He lifted the flip skirt.

"Stop that!"

Pretend I'm your boyfriend looking you over. Is that what you'd say to him?"

"N-n-no."

"Of courts not. You'd just giggle to encourage him." He walked to the front, got eye-level with her breasts, studying them intently, rubbing his chin as he inspected her. He turned to Miss Kusawa and Michiko who were watching him carefully. He placed a cupped hand under one of Suki's breast, eliciting a eking gasp and a bright red response from the girl.

Kuno turned to the two women. "This is advertising. It yells out to a man: 'look-at-me!' Men know an invitation when they see one and this says, "*Ecchizuki*! 'I have no self-esteem, come jump on my bones!' Somehow, it just lacks the subtlety, the mystery, and the uncertainty. The man needs to think: 'is she flirting with me or am I being a pervert for thinking she is?' No, it needs something… something." He looked down at her breast and then up at Suki's face, which was seething behind beet red. "Ah, I think I know what she needs!" He ran off into the underwear section and started to rummage around. "Ah ha! Found it!" He ran back and placed a silk camisole across her chest. "There, now without the bra and with just the *baba-shatsu* she can play hide-and-seek with his eyes!"

The two women stared dumbfounded at Kuno and then looked over at each other before breaking out in applause.

"He's absolutely right! It's the corruptible innocence ploy with a twist!" Miss Kusawa beamed. "Bravo, Kuno!"

"He's a pervert genius!" Michiko added admiringly.

Miss Kusawa leaned over to Michiko, whispering. "Are you sure he's straight?"

Kuno glared, "I heard that!"

Michiko thought for a moment.

Kuno was stunned. "Michiko-chan! Do you really have to think about it?"

She looked at Kuno while answering Miss Kusawa. "Well, your boobs did turn him into putty. And from what I could see under the desk, he had a very… straight response to your advances." She pointed upward with her finger.

Miss Kusawa was gleeful. "Oh, it's so good to know that I can still do that to the boys. However, the dread day will come when I must rely on teaching skills to hold their attention." She shook her head. Looking back at Kuno and Suki, she said, "Okay, we'll take it!"

Look at me

After what they went through shopping with Kuno the night before, Michiko figured that Suki should at least give it a test run.

Suki put on the sheer blouse with the camisole under and no bra but went with a slightly longer, pleated skirt and nylons, a garter belt and the pink frilly panties beneath. Miss Kusawa referred to this outfit as the 'Introductory peep show'. Michiko helped Suki make herself up and prepared her newly colored hair. For an added flair, because Ted was so much taller, she wore high heels to make her look taller and slimmer.

She wore the outfit to school to show Miss Kusawa and to get some practice in walking with high heels. The motions of her breasts swaying under the camisole took some getting used to and the sensation against the silky material made her nipples stiff.

She turned to Michiko, "I pray that no one will notice."

Michiko looked around at the boys on the quad.

"Everyone's noticing."

Michiko sat at the table studying as Suki came through the dorm room door that evening. She waited for Suki to close the door before pouncing. "How did it go?"

"Well, okay, I guess." Suki placed her bag down next to the door.

Michiko frowned. "That wasn't a rhetorical question; I want details!"

Suki pulled up a place on the floor at the table and got comfortable.

"By the time I got to work, I was moving naturally. The skirt was flipping up to expose the top of my stockings and garter belt and the gentle swaying of my breasts no longer felt awkward. I had gotten into their rhythm.

"When I walked in it was business as usual he didn't take his eyes off of the computer and I went to work over at my computer across the room. I greeted him and he said 'hi' and waved without looking in my direction. Our relationship has evolved into a comfortable intellectual rut.

"But I was determined that today was going to be different. It had to be."

"So what did you do then?" Michiko asked.

"I set up my compact mirror next to the monitor so I could see him without turning around. Then I set my legs into a pose hiked up my skirt high enough to show the top of the nylons and the garter strap, just as I rehearsed it with you and Miss Kusawa.

"He never turned around. Later, I coughed a few times like I was clearing my throat."

Michiko hung on every word. "Did that get his attention?"

"A little. He asked if I was okay. I told him I just had a dry throat. He suggested I get some water from the refrigerator. So, I took the opportunity to try to get him to look at me. I went to the little refrigerator where he keeps his drinks in and instead of squatting when I opened it; I bent over at the waist."

"Oh, good move. Did everything show? Were his eyes popping?"

"He didn't move. I got the water and went back to my seat. He asked if I was better now and I said, 'Yes, thank you'. It's hard to read him."

"So, he never once looked at you? What a waste of trampy womanhood! Typical man!"

"Well not exactly. After an hour of his ignoring me, I came across a word on the blog that was new to me. As Ted always told me, 'when in doubt, look it up'. I looked around for the dictionary. I asked him where it was and he said he had put it up on the shelf that morning after using it. I looked up at the top shelf and reached up to get it but could not quite reach it. I stretched and stood on my tiptoes. I was able to get the book to move with my fingertips. I must have made sounds like I was straining because he finally looked over at me while everything was showing halfway up my panties. My white thighs and part of my butt cheeks were popping out. The panties were giving me a wedgie, so I know he got an eyeful. The book was giving away and falling down and it was bringing another with it. I cringed, waiting for it to hit me on the head.

"I heard, 'Look out!" and felt Ted's arms pull me into his chest to protect me as he reached up and caught the books. I know that I planned for him to notice me but to feel the clutch of his strong arms gripping me still came as a shock. Then he looked down at me and handed me the dictionary. As he did, I saw his eyes lock onto my breasts under the blouse and the camisole. The excitement made my nipples hard and they popped out. He quickly averted his eyes like a gentlemen and he mumbled that I should be more careful and use the step stool next time. After that I watched him in my mirror and every few minutes he stole a glance my way."

Michiko rubbed her hands together in delicious satisfaction. "So, phase one is a success. What now?"

The knock at the gate came out of the cool still darkness of the early morning and since it was so faint, Suki feared no one would hear and knocked harder. She stood there wearing another of Miss Kusawa and Kuno's fashion statements. A short schoolgirl style flip skirt, high stockings, a loose halter blouse over a camisole, lacier and sheerer than the one she wore on the previous day. She had a scarf draped around her shoulders over her breasts and was again braless.

"Suki? What are you doing here this early?" Ted stood smiling in the entrance to the yard wearing a black tank top and dogi pants with a black belt bearing red stripes around his waist. Holding the gate open he wiped sweat from his face with a towel draped around his neck.

Suki could not help but notice that if you covered up his face, Ted had the body of a much younger man or did his body have the face of an older man? She couldn't quite tell. "I-I'm sorry to disturb you at this early hour, but I was frantic that my phone was lost. I think I might have left it here!"

"Oh, it's no problem, go right in. Excuse my appearance; I was in the middle of my morning workout."

Suki moved past him with an apologetic bow as she ducked under the arch his arm formed over the door. She trotted across the yard as she and Michiko practiced, with just enough of a flirty swish to her skirt to be innocently provocative.

She removed her shoes and bent down to pick them up. Straps from her garter belt held up her stockings and the sheer black lace panties offered a suggestion of what lay beneath. She didn't have to turn around to know where his eyes were. She hopped up the steps and disappeared around the corner towards Ted's room. Once inside, she reached into her purse and pulled out her phone. As quietly made her way back out

From the porch of the boarding house, Suki observed Ted. She watched Ted resume his exercises with a rhythmic fashion. But, after months of spying on him, she could tell his concentration was disturbed. Now that could be a sign that she was distracting him in either a good or a bad way. She watched as he stopped, refocused his stance and began again. The fluidity of his movement was intrinsic. It was obvious that he had practiced for many years. He was mannish and powerful, yet buoyant and responsive. There was a sexual appeal from his physique, his bearing, his unassuming and respectful way around people, and his humility. When she passed him coming in, she caught a whiff of musky tartness that a man exudes in the straining of exercise… or in the throes of sex. It is a pleasant fragrance, quite exhilarating. She could now see what the other woman found attractive about Ted.

Suki mood turned dark.

The image of that woman, fresh from a bath, wearing his robe, her hair still dripping wet, carrying tea to him – it made Suki bite her lower lip. She knew it was jealousy; it haunted her since she saw them that day. She had stood here, where Suki now stood, watching him workout, loving him with her eyes and with her body.

Suki trembled. Her hand stiffened around her phone and if her teeth clenched any tighter on her lip, she would draw blood. Her chest grew heavy and hollow; she felt her eyes mist over. She could not let him see her like this. She headed past him rushing towards the gate, her head turned away. A cool breeze caught her hair and mercifully blew it across her eyes as the wind caused a tear to stream along her face.

He called out to her. "Uh, did you find your phone?"

Suki held it up for him to see. She left through the gate and headed down the street.

Ted went to the gate and looked after her. "I'll see you this afternoon then?" He gave her back a half wave.

Suki looked over her shoulder and returned his wave. "Okay. At three."

Michiko looked at Suki, who rested in the chair across from her on the balcony. "After you left, he just went inside and didn't finish his routine. I think your visit spooked him. Why did you run out so quick?"

"I couldn't breathe. I thought of that woman being with him and my emotions swelled to the point where I thought I'd choke." Suki, splayed in her chair fanning her face despite the chill in the air, said, "I can't believe I've let another woman come between us, before there even is an 'us'!"

Michiko let the binoculars she had used to watch the encounter dangle by the strap. "So, what's your plan for the other woman?"

"I have to get Ted away from her… or her away from him; I have to get her out of my head!" Suki rolled her head along the back of the chair and cast an eye towards Michiko from beneath the hair blown across her face. "I have to kill her."

Michiko began to laugh, thinking it was a joke. Suki's dark, vacant eyes staring back out of a placid face made her shiver, but not from the cold.

Schemers

"A rival?" Miss Kusawa seemed taken aback at Suki's revelation. "Oh, well, now that changes everything."

Michiko sat on a desktop swinging her legs and licking at a lollipop, which was mesmerizing Kuno. "Suki's going to kill her." She announced it with a blasé tone, as though she were answering a rote test question, never taking her attention off her sucker.

Miss Kusawa looked over at Michiko and then to Suki, sulking in the desk next to her. "Okay, that's one solution…" Miss Kusawa added, "Just not the cleanest means of solving the problem. After all, she'd be dead but you'd be in jail. No, it's not workable. You'll have to come up with something else."

Kuno couldn't stop staring at Michiko. "You really know how to work that thing."

"A girl's got to stay in practice."

Kuno spoke as his eyes watch Michiko. "How about if Suki just seduces him like a cheap whore?"

"Why did you think of that while watching me?" Michiko pointed the sucker at him. "Want some?"

"I mean if this woman is seducing Suki's man, then Suki should go and all out to seduce him first." He stuck his tongue out to Michiko. "Pweeze!"

"Aren't the outfits having any affect?" Miss Kusawa looked a bit disappointed.

Suki raised her hands from her folded arms. "Oh yes, he's noticing me, but if this woman shows up again, she may have an advantage. She seems to be older and probably much more experienced than me."

"Your man's into older women?"

Anxious glances passed between the three students.

Kuno finally spoke. "He's not your type, Miss Kusawa."

"That's not what I was getting at, Kuno!" Flustered and blushing Miss Kusawa defended herself. "Besides, how would you know my type? And if you say that you're my type, I'll…"

"Spank me?" There was a note of hope in his voice.

"You are one twisted little puppy! No, much worse: I'll begin buttoning my blouse to the top during class."

"No! Anything but that! You make English class fun."

"So wiseass, who's my type?"

"Beefcake with brains?" Michiko offered.

"Exactly!" Kuno looked at Miss Kusawa and grinned.

"Mr. Suzuki!"

Miss Kusawa's eyes widened and she blushed. "The Assistant Science professor? Suzuki-san? Well isn't he kinda…"

Kuno said, "Geeky? You need a man who'll stimulate more than your body."

"No." Miss Kusawa said. "I like the geeky, bookish types."

"Shy? You're a control freak and probably a closet dominatrix." Michiko leered as she pointed the sucker at her teacher.

"Mmmm, no. I adore shy guys."

"Short?" Kuno asked. "He's a head and a half shorter than you."

"Hopefully, not where it counts."

"Aha, then that brings us to manly? Michiko offered. "He works out at the gym after work every day."

Kuno said, "Think of Mr. Suzuki's head on Bruce Lee's body."

Miss Kusawa licked her lips as she closed her eyes.

Michiko waved her hands for Miss Kusawa to stop. "No, no! Erase that image from your mind! We can't have you losing control here!"

"But every guy I date has something that kills the relationship. He's not homo is he?"

"No!" Kuno laughed. "When you pass by he gets so hot his glasses fog up and he walks into walls. He has to carry his books low for an hour."

Michiko looked at Kuno. "Carry his books low? Why?"

Kuno gestured to his crotch.

"Oh to cover his…" Michiko screwed up her face. "Eeww! That's so…"

"Flattering!" Miss Kusawa smiled. "The sincerest compliment a man can give a woman's body is a boner."

"And you call me twisted!" Kuno said.

"We're forgetting that we all came here to help Suki's love life, not mine." Miss Kusawa looked at Suki, who had her head falling back as if she might be asleep. "So tell me Suki does your body give your man a boner?"

"What?" Suki's head shot up and she stared wide-eyed at Miss Kusawa.

"Does he desire your body?"

"I-I haven't asked him."

"Does he display any signs that he's aroused when you're around? Has he changed any habits?"

"Well he has been glancing at me more often, and he smiles more than he did when we first met."

"No changes down south?" Miss Kusawa asked.

She blushed and played with her fingers. "Oh, I never noticed. We're not yet at that stage."

"Sounds like you need to pick up the pace if you're going to compete with the rival woman."

"Besides you, what kind of women is he attracted to?"

"I don't know. He has very few pictures in his home. But the other woman is tall and has long hair."

From behind Miss Kusawa, Michiko gave Suki a signal to change the subject.

"I think there was someone once, but I don't know anything about her."

"Hmm, you need to go on a fact-finding mission."

"Why?"

"To find out what type of woman turns him on and then, become that woman."

"How do I do that?"

"Become a spy!"

Suki followed Ted's routine and observed.

Ted was a creature of habit: His morning routine was to exercise after a night of writing and emailing his publishers overseas, take a bath and get six hours of sleep. After waking around noon, he walked to the market to buy his daily needs and stop to have coffee and read a newspaper at a local café. After reading, he would simply stare out the window and watch people go by. Back in his office he prepared for work by sorting and trying to arrange the papers he would need to begin his day. Then he would take a bowl of rice and place it in front of Miko's shrine, light incense and say a prayer. This was no longer a life; it was the remnant of his existence.

For her to look around it would have to be when he was going to be out for a long time, at least an hour. She timed his marketing and breakfast coffees and found that it gave her a two-hour window. Now she only needed a premise to be alone in his room.

"Ted?"

"Yes?" He answered her without looking back her way.

"For the next blog, can I write the content on my experience of the cross-cultural effects on the native speaker?"

He thought for a moment and turned in his seat to look at her. "Its a topic that I certainly can't cover being the alien speaker. I guess one reason I'm having trouble finding topics is because its mostly one sided." He looked at her for a moment.

Suki was hoping he would say yes. It was part of her thesis and she had ample materials to cover her while she searched his apartment for clues. As she watch him watching her she got the distinct feeling he was lingering on her long bare legs and her exposed thigh and ogling… Ted was unconsciously ogling her! It made her happy and she bathed in his gaze.

"I think that it would be an excellent idea. It will breathe new life into the blog to have a fresh perspective."

"So it won't interfere with my regular work, maybe I can come by early on Friday to get it started. Say, around 12?

My professor's at a conference and I have the time off - if it won't be a bother."

"Oh, no noon Friday's fine. I'll be expecting you then."

Come Friday, Suki once again stood before Ted's gate. Again the warm winds played with her skirt, exposing the suggestion of tiny blue panties that covered less than her previous ones. Next in the plan would be a thong for a better butt shot, then maybe – nothing! For now she took her image change in the stages suggested by Miss Kusawa. A whistle came from behind her and some workers were showing their approval. Before, she would have been embarrassed and pulled her skirt tight. She just gave them a shy smile and turned her face back to the gate, letting the wind have its way with her. Out of their sight, her shy smile turned to a subtle beam of sinful satisfaction.

Mr. Hideo opened the gate to see her head bowed slightly with a demure smile on her lips. "Why hello, Suki. You're early today. Is Ted expecting you?"

"Oh yes, we have a project that I'm starting on today."

"Well, He usually sleeps until noon, or one, so I don't know if he's up yet. I can go wake him if you like."

"Its okay, I'll check on him myself. He may have forgotten about the time. He's like that."

After leaving Hideo-san, she walked softly up to Ted's door and knocked gently. No response. Then she knocked a little louder. Still, there was no response. She gently slid the panel back and peeked inside. She placed her bag down and took put her shoes down. She moved the panel back enough to enter and listened for Ted. She heard snoring coming from around the corner in his living area and figured he had forgotten the time. She walked over and looked around to where Ted was sleeping. She saw him on the floor shirtless, wearing thin cotton pajama bottoms with a pillow pulled over his head to block the daylight. As her eyes adjusted she saw a lump under the pajamas: quite a generous one. It was how all healthy boys woke up in the morning. Ted was certainly healthy in that department. Suki wondered who he was dreaming about, her or the other woman? It was pointing upwards towards his stomach where Suki had an unobstructed view of the scars he carried from the accident that killed his wife. They were as healed as they would ever be, permanent reminders of his past life, Suki stared at the scars and imagined the pain they represented. How he suffered. It saddened her. How she just wanted to reach out and caress those scars and kiss their pain away. A single tear ran down her cheek as she reached for his body and then drew back in horror of being discovered. She quickly left with her shoes and bag and went outside to knock again until he answered the door.

He came to the door. "Oh, Suki! Sorry, I must have forgot you were coming and overslept. Please go right in and make yourself comfortable. I'll be right back, I have to go to the bathroom."

Suki looked admiringly down at his bulge, everything clearly displayed through the sheer cotton material of his pajamas, backlit by a reflection on the floor. "Yes, I can see that." She strolled past him into the room, smiling.

Seeking Out the Past

A fully dressed Ted came out of his room. "Sorry about earlier Suki, I-I just woke up and came to the door without thinking. Sorry if it embarrassed you."

She smiled at him and gently opened her fan. "It seems that you were the one more embarrassed. Don't worry it just means you're still healthy and that is a good thing, isn't it?

"Well, yeah, I guess…" Changing the subject he said, "I have to go out to the market and for breakfast. Will you be all right until I return?"

"Yes. In fact I've already started the first paragraph." She showed him the screen.

"Is there anything you need or that I can bring you?"

"Oh, no. I'm fine. Thank you."

He left and she heard his steps walking down the hall. She leaned back in the chair exhausted. "I'm burning up! That was so hot!" She fanned her face and then pulled her blouse out and fanned her chest. "Now I know what the other girls in high school meant by joking they had bananafish congee for breakfast!" Then she reached down and lifted her skirt, spreading her legs she fanned furiously. "I've got to cool down! I'm on a mission!"

Just then she heard the footsteps outside the door and regained her composure and faked working before Ted popped his head back into the room. "Oh, I forgot to tell you that there's plenty of juice in the refrigerator if you get thirsty. She turned to him from her work and gave him a cute smile. "Oh, thank you. I think I'll have some later." Ted nodded, smiled and left again. She kept her post waving to him with the cute smile plastered on her face until he was by the gate. "I am sooo glad I always carry dry panties in my purse."

She waited for a while until she heard the gate shut and was sure he was gone to the market. The she reached into her purse and pulled out a flash drive and plugged it into the port. She downloaded the complete paper so she would have something to show when he returned. Then she got to work.

She first went over to his living area out of sight of the front door to change her damp panties. She slipped out of the wet ones and left them on the floor as she put on the dry ones. As she picked them up she spotted this pillows and his futon stacked in the corner. She walked over and picked up his pillows and wiped her panties on them. "Let's see who you dream about tonight."

Then she placed the panties in a small bag and put them in her purse. She looked around to see where he might have personal items, like pictures of girls that he liked, including her rival.

She opened drawers and took pictures of things before rummaging around so she could match it up again when she was finished.   That was Kuno's suggestion.   There was nothing in the bottom drawers. She went through the closet and saw something on the top shelf. It was too high to reach so she brought a stool over and pulled it down. There were photo albums and some videocassettes with a lot of dust on them. She took it down and put everything on the stool.

She opened the photo albums and saw pictures of Ted with a pretty woman, Miko, his wife. They were playing with two children a girl and boy. They were in their home and out in the garden. She kept turning and saw them at the beach. She noticed that they were always together and there were no pictures of friends or gatherings for either the parents or the children. It made her sad for them to be left out of society.

She began taking pictures of Miko as she went along. In the next album she found more of the same kind of pictures many with Ted hugging Miko and kissing her and always smiling for the camera. Suki noticed that he smiled a lot then.   Miko had a seductive presence when facing the camera as Ted took her picture. Occasionally, she would pull down a blouse and bra strap and wink. This was a good one for her to photograph. He seemed to like it since she did it a lot. In the last one a small envelope fell out and the pictures spilled out of it as it hit the floor. They were more recent and in them Miko was sometimes naked and posing for the camera. She had a very nice body, more stacked than Suki, but not too much more. She had a flawless complexion and no blemishes on her skin. Suki took out her camera and photographed each photo in the bag before returning them to their original position. She could study them later. As she put everything back where she had found it, the videos caught her eye. There were about three dozen, and by the look of them he rarely watched them. She decided to take three for viewing. Since they were by date she took an early one and the latest one and one that was lettered in red from among half a dozen similarly marked ones.

She searched for photos or mementos of the other woman but found none.

With everything back in place, she looked around to see what other items might give her a clue to Ted's personality. In his personal area, aside from the photos and videos there was nothing. Outside of his work, he had no personality. She went back to the office and wandered about looking for something to give her a hint of his interests.

At the end of the room she came to Miko's shrine. She knelt in front of the shrine and stared at the photo of the dead woman who occupied so much of Ted's heart. She was very pretty and playful with a little bit of private scandal in the mix. "Who were you Miko? Why did Ted love you so much that he still mourns you so after so long? She reached over and touched her picture with reverence. "I am Suki. I am your replacement. I will take very good care of Ted, I promise. You must promise me something. You must promise to let go of Ted so he can let go of you.

Promise me that you will... die forever!" With that, she pushed the photo over and it fell to the floor.

Ted returned and began his routine; He placed his papers in order and then went into the kitchen for a small bowl of rice to offer to Miko. He knelt, lit the incense and placed the rice before her picture. He assumed the prayer position and began to pray. He was oblivious to Suki working in the background. From time-to-time the picture of Miko would peek out in the mirror next to Suki's computer and taunt her. Her eyes were telling Suki that Ted was still hers and that she would take him to the grave with her.

Later in the afternoon, Suki announced she was finished with the draft and asked if he would like to see it. He told her that she could give him a hard copy, but Suki unplugged the printer so it couldn't work. It made Ted get up and go over to her computer. She pushed the screen up so he could read it by standing over her. Behind her he looked down at the screen, then she leaned back in her chair a bit letting him see down her blouse and her braless breasts beneath. Her scent was Thai Rose, the most exotic fragrance she could afford on her student's stipend. Occasionally she would lean back and look up at him to explain her thesis. It had the desired effect when her head 'accidently' brushed his crotch. It was one of Miss Kusawa's lessons in seduction. Demonstrating to Suki how it worked, she put Kuno in a narrow place and squeezed by, rubbing up against him by 'accident'. Then she dropped her pencil and backed into him by 'accident' again. When she turned around to see her handiwork she patted Kuno's chin and thanked him for his 'compliment'.

"It's very, very good, Suki. Just tighten it up a little and go ahead and post it under your by-line. I'd like to see more. As he began to walk over to his desk she asked him if he would mind having her work on it here since she could ask him questions? He turned sideways to answer her and she saw the bulge had returned to his pants. "Sure. That would be fine." He returned to his seat and she noticed him rearranging himself as he sat down.

"Ted, thank you for the compliment. It means a lot to me."

Suki had the videos transferred to digital formats and placed them on flash drives for safekeeping. She was then able to replace the originals without Ted ever being aware that they were gone.

On Saturday night, she opted not to go out with Michiko and stayed home to analyze the videos and photos she had copied. First she downloaded all the photos she had onto her computer. She went through the photos of Ted as a young man and Miko with their small children. She noticed that Ted liked to catch Miko in sexy poses or make candid shots of her when she was not aware he was there. Mostly shooting her from the back and sometimes focused on her butt. "Maybe he's a butt man." Suki stripped down to her underwear and used a small mirror to see her backside in the full-length mirror. She tried to mimic the poses of Miko. She took photos of herself in the mirror in various poses that she saw Miko strike. Then she brought up the photos she took from the envelope that had dropped out.

She brought up a nude standing shot of Miko. She took off her panties and bra and took her photo standing in the same pose. She downloaded it and brought it up next to Miko's for a comparison. Miko had larger breasts, but their hips seemed about the same. Miko was shaved clean and Suki had a pleasant bush, thick but not too big, though it could use a trim. In the next one she was shot from behind, again, Suki matched her features for roundness and plumpness. Obviously, Miko was open to experimenting if the photos were any indication. She watched the videos the oldest being early in their marriage on a vacation at the beach. She saw how they played with their small children and how in the water Miko let her top down for the camera. "Ah-ha, she teases him with peeks! That is probably why he responded to me the other day. Ted, you're a dirty old voyeur."

The next video was at a festival, wearing traditional yukata. He filmed her walking around with her hair up, prim in a very traditional sense. She looked around and then back at the camera with a wink, and then she hiked up her yukata to show him her bare ass. "She liked the danger of flashing him in public places." He chased her with the camera. "I wonder if he did her in the yukata. "Whoa!" Suki's eyes grew big as she watched the video. "That answers that question!" She watched with a mix of revulsion and fascination for the next hours, as they got rough and frenzied with one another in the videos.

The next morning she came out on the balcony with Michiko and sat in her chair. "Oww, She made a grimace and repositioned herself gingerly on the chair.

Michiko smirked. "Fun night?"

Suki just glared at her.

"I've got to see those videos. Oh, by the way, did you know there's a Fireworks Festival coming up next week in the park near the shrine and—"

"Quick, Michiko, where can I get a yukata!?!"

Suki's Stratagem

The department store was not crowded for a Sunday morning. Michiko walked with Suki along the aisle of the traditional wear section where kimonos, hakamas and yukatas were sold; pointing out unusual patterns she thought might look nice on Suki.

Suki was looking too, but with the aid of pictures she had brought along. She kept nixing Michiko's suggestions: She obviously had something specific in mind. Scanning the racks she spotted something picked it up and held it aloft, scrutinized it, and comparing it to her reference materials. She shook her head and returned it. Her behavior baffled Michiko. Finally, she seemed to find something and pulled it from the rack. "Michiko, please hold this up on you so I can get a better look at it."

Michiko spread the yukata out and draped it in front of her as Suki took a few steps back to assess the robe. Suki looked at the robe and then to the picture. Then she took the picture and held it up to compared the two. "Not a perfect match, but very, very close. I'll try it on."

In the dressing room mirror Suki was scrutinizing three

views of herself. Each gave her a different view of her body as he might see it when she wore the yukata to the festival. Michiko found it peculiar that her expression was not the happy face a girl gets when finding something she likes, but more of a critical assessment of a thing she might find useful. Then again, Suki was a peculiar girl.

"It has to be perfect." her face was wrinkled in self-criticism and concentration. Returning a smile to her face, she turned to show Michiko.

Michiko wasn't keen on it. "It looks good, but don't you think that pattern is kind of old for you? It makes you look, well, mature."

Suki ignored her and looked over her shoulder to the backside, tugging the yukata a bit to show off more of her shape. "Well, I am trying to impress an older man. I think this is something he will respond to." She looked at her reflection in the mirror full on. "Yes, Ted will like this. It's perfect! I'll take it."

Michiko spied Suki's reflection in the mirror and saw how her eyes glistened in an unsettling way as she inspected the gown over her slim body. A tiny, wicked smile crossed her face and the effect made Michiko uneasy.

After convincing Michiko to buy a yukata of her own to wear to the festival, the girls headed out of the department store.

"Suki I couldn't help but notice that you didn't buy any underwear designed for your yukata."

"Don't you know its traditional not to wear anything

underneath a yukata? I'm going commando!"

"Wow, our shy Suki is getting bold! So, what's next on your seduction list?"

"Next?" She laughed. "I go and get a full body wax."

"Full body? You mean all your hair?"

"Yep every one must go. My skin needs to be smooth, like a baby's."

Michiko pointed to her own crotch. "Even down there?"

Suki looked to where she was pointing and then up to Michiko's eyes and turned straight ahead with that same conspiratorial gaze and smirk. "Especially down there."

"That's kind of creepy, Suki. I didn't know Ted was into lolitots."

After the waxing, Michiko asked Suki how she felt

"Smooth, tender…" She looked down, inside her pants. "And a little naked."

Michiko laughed. "What now?"

"Now this." She held out a photo of a woman with her face violently blotted out with a broad tipped marker. The woman's hair was the only part Suki had left untouched.

Michiko smiled uneasily. "You didn't have to go to that extreme, did you?"

Suki inspected her handiwork on the printout. "I wanted to imagine my face there, to get a feel for the hair."

"Its retro. Kinda eighties looking. It's longer than your

own hair so I don't think it'll work."

They arrived at the beauty parlor and Suki opened the door. "Haven't you heard of hair extensions?"

That evening Michiko insisted on a fashion show and Suki was happy to oblige.

Michiko called out to Suki changing in the bathroom. "I'm going to look at that video you were watching last night, all right?"

"Okay." Suki called from the bathroom.

As she set up Suki's notebook, she called, "Hey, do you think Ted will be at the festival?"

"I already asked him, he said he'd go with me?"

"How'd you convince him?"

"I told him I could give him a native's perspective that he might otherwise not get by simply observing?"

"Why you clever girl! Appealing to his raw intellect, nice!" After a moment Michiko got a thought that she couldn't keep inside. "Say Suki, do you think there's anything else raw and appealing about Ted?"

Suki called from the bathroom. "Watch the video. Then you tell me if there is."

Michiko opened up the video of Ted and Miko at the festival, watching it from where Suki had queued the best parts, where Ted had Miko's yukata opened up.

That got her attention. "Oooh…"

Ted and Miko had stolen away behind a building and to make passionate love. He had placed the camera down on a nearby rock to catch all the action.

"It all looks so… kama sutra with them wearing traditional robes. I stand corrected – not wearing them! "Wow!" Michiko's eyes popped open. "Did you see him hoist her up in mid air and drop her down?   They're freaking acrobats! She began licking her lips calling out to her roommate. "Hey, Suki! Do you think he's still strong enough to do that?"

"I intend to find out." She leaned her head out of the bathroom and grinned. "Don't you think it would be a beautiful way for me to lose my flower?"

Michiko watched the video. "If this is an example of his lust, he'll have you walking bowlegged for a week!"

Suki entered the room making minor adjustments to the robe. "So what do you think?" She wore the yukata with a yellow sash, and her hair was tied in double ponytails and with bangs over her forehead while random hairs hung down the around her shoulders and back.   The hair extensions made her look like a different woman.

The transition that the yukata made to Suki impressed Michiko. She began to compliment her on how pretty she looked. "Wow, you look stunning! It looks great Suki, just like…" Michiko looked from Suki to the computer screen; the close similarity between the yukatas both were wearing gave her clarity as to Suki's scheme. She noted that with her hair extensions, Suki had replicated Miko's hair. Even down to the fine, hairless crotch, Suki had become a copy of Miko. She had brought a dead woman back from the ashes.

"What are you trying to do, Suki?" Michiko challenged her roommate. "This isn't funny!"

"Funny?" Suki glided towards Michiko. Her head cocked like a puppy hearing a strange sound for the first time. "But Michiko it is funny."

Suki halted in front of Michiko, who was lying on the floor where she had been looking at the computer. With the light next to Michiko shining up into her face, Suki had the countenance of an evil kabuki doll, staring down at her, with her head still tilted in amusement. "Isn't it funny how Ted continues to mourn Miko?"

Suki raised her head and gazing out of the window, her voice floated into the darkness beyond the balcony. "Why does he still yearn for Miko: a dead, cold corpse, when he can have a warm, young, vital women like me? Don't you think it's funny, Michiko?"

Suki slid along the floor – barely rustling the hem of her gown – and out onto the balcony placing one hand delicately on the railing, clutching the opening of her robe with the other, staring down at the courtyard below where Ted worked out every morning. "No matter what I do to try and get his attention as Suki, it's never going to be enough."

Michiko's voice was small and low, as though she feared agitating Suki. "So what is it you have planned?"

Still staring down into the courtyard below, Suki smiled

sweetly. This smile seemed disjointed, out of place on her innocent face, like a postmortem grimace. "If Ted cannot see me because he wants to see only his dead wife," Suki turned to Michiko with the same smile, and her eyes had a strange, dead emptiness to them, as though it was no longer sweet little Suki speaking. "Then for him to see me I must become Miko." The sound of her voice deepened and seemed much older.

"Miko?" She croaked out the question. Fear crawled into Michiko's throat. "You want to become Miko?"

"Of course. After all…" Suki looked directly at Michiko and lowered her voice almost to a whisper.

"…Miko is the first one I must kill."

Festival Surprise

This festival was the prefecture's major annual event. Since the shrine and park were located so close to the university, students always looked forward to making the Fireworks Festival a school break event. Tonight, the crowds had gathered tightly to watch the opening ceremonies, including the beating of the taiko drums to usher in the new moon. The game and arcade booths were two and three deep in chattering, happy people. Many girls shrieked in alarm at a goosing when passing boys and frustrated by not being able to tell which one in the thick crowd had touched her. Many girls and boys dressed in fine yukatas and locating each other would be difficult, so the roommates arranged to meet at the base of the shrine stairs. Michiko and Kuno arrived first. Suki soon followed.

"Do you think Ted will like this?" Suki squirmed with excitement as she showed off her robe and new look to Michiko.

Michiko was more reserved, but managed to muster a

convincing smile. "If the video's any indicator, he'll eat you up."

"I hope so."

"Where did you tell him to meet us?"

"Here at the stairs. At six-thirty."

Ted arrived promptly at six-thirty wearing a hakama that was more formal than the one he wore while working out.

Suki said to Michiko, "Doesn't he look handsome tonight?"

He passed right by them, looking around in the crowd for the shorthaired Suki and Michiko. He spotted Kuno, whom he knew from seeing him walking the girl's home. "Hello Kuno. Have you seen Suki?"

"She's right behind you."

Ted turned and almost skipped over Suki again, looking for the shorthaired girl he knew. His eyes stopped abruptly on Suki. His face became drawn, confused and pale, uncertain of what he was seeing. He looked like he'd seen… a ghost. He said nothing, only stared at Suki.

Michiko jumped into his line of site wearing her yukata and wearing her hair the same way. "Surprise! How do you like us? We're retro girls from the 90's!"

Ted blinked a bit and tried to grasp what Michiko was saying. "Oh, I see. Is this some kind of cosplay for the festival?"

Suki smiled at Ted with a shy seductiveness, while letting

Michiko do all the talking.

"Yes, that's it! We saw these outfits in an old magazine and thought we'd try to look like them."

Ted warmed up to the idea a little. "Well you certainly got the look down. Very authentic."

Suki held out her arms and whirled around so he could appreciate her from the back. "Do you think it's too much? I even had my hair done in the style of an 90's woman. "

"That yukata, its, its…

Suki began to panic.

"It's so attractive! I don't think I've seen one like it before. It looks good on you, like it was made just for you."

Suki blushed as she moved closer to Ted. "Thank you Ted, it is very sweet of you to say such nice things."

Michiko let out an audible sigh of relief. Suki looked her way and smiled.

Kuno leaned over and whispered into Michiko's ear. Her face lost its color as she looked down the path and among the crowd; she saw Miss Kusawa and Mr. Suzuki approaching the shrine stairs.

Ted had his back to the approaching couple, but Suki saw them even before the others told her. She looked up at Ted, moved to his side, and took his arm. "I saw something on my way here that we can discuss in terms of the native versus alien observation perspective." She pulled him along as she spoke. "After all, we came here to make observations. Work, work, work! We can have fun later."

She escorted him off in a rush.

"Well, okay. Bye guys!" Ted smiled and waved to Kuno and Michiko as Suki dragged him off.

Michiko and Kuno positioned themselves to head off Miss Kusawa and Mr. Suzuki before they could spot Suki with Ted. Not waiting for them to recognize her and Kuno, she called out to the couple. "Hi Miss Kusawa, Professor Suzuki, Its nice to see you here. What a pleasant surprise!" Michiko looked at Kuno who just shrugged. Neither knew that she would be attending the festival, certainly not with Professor Suzuki.

As she approached, Miss Kusawa looked a little surprised to find them here. She also looked red and flushed. "Oh, hi!" She forced a smile as she panted out her greeting like she was short of breath.

"Miss Kusawa you look stunning in your kimono. And Professor Suzuki, you look so handsome tonight. What a great couple you make!" It may have sounded like mock flattery, but Michiko was sincere. Miss Kusawa stood a head above him and looked stunning. She glowed and he was, well, a frog that she would kiss and turn into a handsome prince. Together their very appearance was just too cute. "Kawaii!" Michiko squealed. Michiko and Kuno bowed to their seniors. Mr. Suzuki and Miss Kusawa returned the bow.

Miss Kusawa seemed like she was trying to find something to talk about to take her mind off of something else. "Did you manage to find Suki and her boyfriend in this crowd? It's really packed tonight." She glanced at Mr.

Suzuki. "So many people!" Her face became flush again.

He just smiled back. "Indeed, many people to see."

Michiko motioned up the stairs towards the shrine. "They just went to give prayers and make wishes up at the shrine."

Miss Kusawa looked up the steep stairs and gave a weak smile. "Oh, that's nice. I hope they get their wish."

Mr. Suzuki looked up at Miss Kusawa. "Perhaps we too should go upstairs to visit the shrine and make a wish."

"Upstairs?" She looked up the stairs again. "So many stairs! How many do you think there are mast… er, Mr. Suzuki?"

"I do believe that this is one of the shorter temple stairways, only 133 steps."

"133 steps?" She was almost whining a plea not to go up.

"Come my dear, you can lean on me if you get tired." They started up the stairs.

Kuno called out. "Professor, may I have a moment?"

Mr. Suzuki made his apologies to Miss Kusawa and went to Kuno. "Yes?"

"About our agreement?" Kuno whispered, thinking no one would hear, but Michiko was a master eavesdropper. "That grade will be taken cared of won't it?"

Mr. Suzuki whispered back and smiled. "You delivered her as promised. Consider it done." The two men parted.

Miss Kusawa and Mr. Suzuki went up the stairs and Kuno

returned to Michiko's side. He was grinning.

"You 'delivered' Miss Kusawa to him for an improved grade in Mr. Suzuki's class?"

"Yep."

"And you made a perverts deal with Miss Kusawa for setting up the blind date."

"Yep."

"You know, they have a word for that."

"Matchmaker?"

"Pimp."   Then Michiko saw Miss Kusawa stop on the stairs. "She looks exhausted."

"She is. When she bowed, I saw that she was tied up with ropes beneath her robe. Satin ones."

Michiko covered her mouth in shock. "So they really are into S-M? I thought she was a dominatrix."

"No, she's the sub, or submissive, he's the dom, or dominant: Slave and Master. Didn't you catch it when she almost slipped and called him master?"

"Meek little Mr. Suzuki? He is so full of surprises! So, why does she look so exhausted?"

"The bra ropes tighten, pinching and making it harder to breathe. Squeezing the breasts and making her nipples pop out, stimulated as they rub against her silk robes. Then there's the crotch rope knot."

"What? What does that do?"

"Imagine that you're straddling a rope walking up the stairs every third or fourth step a knot in that rope rubs against your crotch. He turned and stood in front of her so no one could see. Rub… rub… pop… rub… rub… pop…"

"Oh!" She flushed and angrily swatted his hand away. "Okay, stop! I get the idea!"

"Imagine it hundreds of times repeating with no relief until the ropes are taken off and you can breathe again. She must have already had a dozen orgasms tonight, and it looks like she's having another. Death by ecstasy!"

"I don't know which is creepier; that she lets him do that to her, or that you know so much about it."

Fireworks

Having narrowly escaped discovery by Miss Kusawa and Mr. Suzuki, Suki peered over her shoulder to see if they were being followed, but at her height and with the crowd so thick, there was no way to tell. She could only hope Michiko and Kuno intercepted them. Suki held tight to Ted's arm under the pretense that her geta sandals were new and slippery, that she did not want to slip and fall. He did not resist her embrace and, in fact, held onto her waist on a particularly steep area. It made Suki happy.

Ted and Suki moved down the hill in the direction the game and food booths. They meandered along the fairway, bought cotton candy, and played games of skill. As she walked the fairway holding Ted's arm, she gazed around at the booths and the colorful lights. The sensation of being with him was the fulfillment of her love.

Dour, unhappy faces glare at her as they pass. Old women disapprovingly gazed, wagging their heads. Men glowered hatefully at Ted, but he did not notice them. He remained oblivious and aloof from years of practice. From the corner of her eye she even saw teenage girls pointing her way and snickering among one another. She tightened her grasp on his arm. They would not stop staring at her, judging her.

At first, it was a small, faint voice. She thought someone nearby was whispering to her. The wispy, little voice told her to look up at Ted.

'Do you want him'? Came the whisper out of the crowd. She recognized the voice from the beta tape: It was Miko's voice.

Glancing up at Ted's face. Her minds own voice answered: 'Yes'.

As if she whispered through the veil of a waterfall, Miko responded, 'Then embrace the harshness of their hateful stares as they shun you. Now you are tainted, no longer pure in their eyes, no longer one of them. Isolation and loneliness are your future. Embrace this sensation every time you hold him. This is your fate for embracing a gaijin. I did… and I am dead.' The voice reverted to sounding like Miss Kusawa's back in the ice cream parlor. 'This is what it is to love a gaijin!'

Suki shivered. Miko being in her head was unsettling. She felt as if she had fever chills and she could not stop shaking. She looked around at the faces and aside from a few glances at him then at her, they no longer seemed hostile. Did she imagine it?

"Are you cold?"

"What?"

"Are you cold? You're shivering."

It must just be the weather. I chill easy. Maybe we should go somewhere quiet so I can sit down for a moment."

They took a path leading away from the crowded fairway towards the restrooms and a small seating area in a side garden. There they found a stone bench to sit on. He helped her sit first and sat at a respectful distance. She continued to shiver as Miko's voice returned to her. 'Do you still want him, knowing all that you must sacrifice to have him?'

Suki sat shivering before closing her eyes tight and answering her with a quiet, 'yes'.

'Then let me come to him through you. I know what it is to love him. I will teach you.'

Suki opened her eyes and looked in the direction of the small voice with misgiving. 'Then he will be yours and not mine'.

Miko gave a short chortle. 'I am dead, so he will be caressing only your warm, living flesh.'

Suki shivered. "Ted, I'm cold, can you hug me to warm me?"

Ted was taken aback by Suki's request, but saw her shivering. "Yes, of course." She sat with her back to him so he placed his arms around her from behind. She felt his warm hands on her deathly cold skin. "You really are cold!"

To bring back her warmth he gave her his body heat; She shivered more as he touched her and moved his arms along her shoulders to warm her: How much of her quivering was from the chill of the night and how much came from his touch, she couldn't tell.

He pulled Suki closer to keep her warm and moved his hands to her arms and shoulders, Suki reached for his hand and guided it beneath the fold of her robe to her waiting breast, her nipples hard with anticipation. He tried to protest by making a feeble attempt to remove his hand but she gripped it tighter holding it in place. Then she reached for his other hand and placed it on her opposite breast.

"Suki- I–I don't think…" She brought her hand up and placed a finger on his lips, hushing him. Though she was no longer holding his hand over her breast, he left it in place.

She looked up at him under the dim festival lanterns, "You think too much." She pulled his head down to her lips. His lips were soft and a pleasant surprise. He kissed her passionately. His hands were timidly massaging her breasts and starting to search for the nipples. It sent an electrical charge down her spine to her womb and her body began trembling in anticipation. She found his tongue and locked it with hers. She sucked his lips with hers. He gave in to her and returned her kisses. He was not like a schoolboy who rushes to get the prize: Ted was experienced; he was slow and gentle, patient and thorough. Her expectations – and his teasing her passions with knowledgeable lips and sure hands made it more agonizingly erotic for her. She hoped that, with all this build up, he could deliver when the time came.

Fireworks burst overhead and everyone's eyes drew skyward but Ted's eyes locked onto Suki, her face and beautiful body exposed by a form fitting yukata. Maybe Ted wanted Suki to be Miko. Maybe he needed to bring her back her memory, just for tonight.

Suki saw her reflection deep in Ted's eye. No, it was not she, but Miko reflection staring back. The twinkle in her eyes and the slight turn of her lips made her look exactly like Miko. Suki was now the woman she wanted him to see – the woman in the memorial picture.

He buried his face into her hair, embracing her tight while kissing her neck. "Miko…"

Ted pulled his face back in horror; he must have realized what he just said. It was Suki, not Miko in his arms. Embarrassed, he tried to pull away. "I'm so sorry, Suki, I just…" He again felt her finger on his lips.

She turned to face him. The top of her robe was loose and her breasts exposed. She giggled. "You talk too much."

She was not offended. He looked relieved. While one hand covered his lips Suki's other hand gently landed flat on his upper chest, beneath his robe, drawing down, exposing his chest.

"You bore such sadness and guilt for far too long." She ran her hand over his burn scars and it made him shudder. "You need to have Miko, to make amends to her, to make love to her. Tonight you need to celebrate your love for her and remember Miko fondly and… tell her goodbye.

"Tonight, I will be Miko for you." She kissed him, pulled away slightly and moved her mouth to his ear. "Love me Ted."

She took his hand in hers and led him along a path to an intimate dark clearing behind the gardeners' shed surrounded by high bushes. She walked this route earlier in the day and this was the best spot for her plan. There was a boulder she sat on and beckoned him to come to and sit next to her. He obliged and she began kissing his face and then his neck and moved down his chest until she reached his scars. She stopped and trembled.

"What's wrong?" Ted asked.

"When I first saw your scars I cried and now I find myself crying again. I want your pain to go away, I want you to be happy again – happy with me.

"You must be happy again..." Suki sobbed and held him tight. "Please Ted, be happy, for me."

Ted held her head against his chest and his scars. Her eyelashes open and closed against his skin and moist tears ran down his stomach. He stroked her hair and comforted her. "Suki, don't worry about me, please. Since you came into my life, my joy has returned. Though I don't say much, I do look forward to when you come to my house."

The fireworks lit her face as she looked up with wet eyes. "Then take me and make your joy complete."

Suki's breath came in short, shallow bursts, preparing for what was next. Her body quivered. Fireworks exploded faster and faster as the show moved towards its finale. Flashing fire in bright colors made him more sensual and desirable. Reds, yellows, and blues crossed his face, giving him a new personality with each burst. A rash of small bursts came as he started to slowly lift her. Her breathing sped up and she could feel her heart thumping against her chest. Suki's mouth was dry from panting and her fingers dug into Ted's skin. She violently arched her back, still gripping hard to Ted's shoulders. Pain: excruciating, unbearable and exquisite pain! Opening her wide eyes upward she peered into the dark sky watching as huge bursts of streamers and multi colored sparkles harmonized with her internal spasms. Tears streamed slowly from the corners of her eyes, the beauty of love's joyous sting! It was wonderful!

She hung around his neck like a talisman, spent and exhausted as he held her. She wished they could just stay here forever, him, together with her as one person.

She moved her head up to his face and instead of kissing him, she nipped his earlobe and French kissed his ear passionately. Suki had no idea why she did it, it was impulsive, but Ted responded immediately to her advance. He buried he head in her neck and her hair and whispered, "Miko!" As she heard him whimper the name, a smile came to her lips and the glint returned to her eyes. Finally, he withdrew and let her down. Why did she do that to Ted? It was not something she thought about or planned, she did it without thinking. It was nice, but it was not like her.

Suki used the lining of her yukata to clean both of them. It surprised her that she bled so much. The lining of the robe absorbed most of it and what seeped through would not be noticeable at night with the dark and intricate design of the yukata.

Since the fireworks were finished they decided to go home. The walk back to Ted's home was quiet and they said very little along the way. She walked in short steps, only as much the getas would allow. As they approached the street where he lived, he held her arm in his out of courtesy and to steady her.

"I, I'm sorry about losing control tonight. It is just that the festival and the fireworks, you looking so… good and I guess… "

Suki brought her hand up to his cheek to calm him. "Don't be sorry for giving me my womanhood and the most wonderful gift of my life. You were incredible back there. I never realized how strong and vital you are. Don't apologize, please."

"Okay, I won't apologize on one condition."

"And that would be?" Suki looked at him curious, smiling.

"That you kiss me now, under this streetlight."

She obliged him, twice. She felt his robes swell at her pressing against him. He still had some energy left. It would be a shame to let it go to waste and end this perfect evening too early.

"Can I ask a favor of you?" Suki whispered as she pulled her lips away. "The dorm bath is not very private and if I bathe there, some of the girls may gossip and spread rumors. May I bathe at your place?"

He smiled, placed his arm around her shoulder, and walked her through the gates of his home.

Mystery Woman

When she arrived home that evening, Michiko found Suki in their room, folding the yukata she'd worn to the festival. Eager to catch up on the gossip, Michiko joined Suki on the floor. She saw the stains on her robe. "Suki-chan the yukata will be hard to clean with all this blood."

"I won't clean it. It is now a sacred garment that I will keep as a memory of the happiest night of my life."

"Are you sure? It was really expensive and you can wear it again."

Suki pointed to a stain. "Look, here I am, and here he is. In the center we come together as one: yin and yang." Her eyes were transfixed on the stain and she gave a smile, pulling the stained fabric to her face, she breathed in. "This is us, the marriage of our selves. Our pent up passions flowed from us, it unleashed these torrents and they are here." She looked at Michiko. "Like a wedding dress: It is only meant to be worn once."

Michiko was concerned for Suki. She had prepared for

this for so long, that now, when it finally happened, something about it was off. She had seen Suki obsessed with Ted before but this was on the verge of sick. "So, how did you convince him?"

She smiled as she finished folding the robe and stood to put it in its box. "It's simple. A man has conjugal rights to his wife's body and may do with it as he wishes."

Michiko was concerned by the waiflike tone in Suki's voice. "But you're not his wife."

"No? No, of course I'm not, not yet, so I had to become the woman he believed to be his wife. For a week, I studied the mannerisms and habits of his wife, Miko. I copied each nuanced move she made; each unconscious gesture became my own. The yukata was as close to the one Miko wore that night and I have a wardrobe of clothes in colors and styles to remind him of her."

Michiko was bewildered. "Why do you want him to think of you as his dead wife? That's just weird."

"With the young, innocent Suki, he may have felt he was taking advantage of a naive country girl. As his Miko, what he did with me is perfectly acceptable; there is no guilt for a man to have sex with his wife. As Miko I am the older and experienced woman that he is familiar with. So I am his Miko." Suki pulled an outfit from her closet and went to the bathroom to change in front of the mirror. She slipped on the one piece dress over her underwear and flipped her long hair out from under the collar. "I even let him call me Miko to complete his fantasy."

Michiko saw a small snapshot of Miko on the mirror,

wearing the exact outfit. "Are you going to take out the hair extensions?"

"Not yet."

"Why not?"

"I will in time so he will start seeing me as me, but for now... " She brushed her locks. "Ted likes my hair like this."

"But it's not your hair, its Miko's"

Suki didn't say anything she just kept brushing her hair. She then placed the brush down and walked past Michiko.

"Where are you going?"

Suki walked over to the door and picked up an overnight bag sitting by the door. "I have to go to work and I promised Ted that I would make him dinner tonight." She lifted the overnight bag over her shoulder. "Don't wait up for me."

"Suki, this is nuts! You can't go on pretending to be Ted's dead wife."

"I have to. It's the only way to kill her in Ted's memory: by being her then changing his perception of me over time." Suki walked to the door and opened it. "I'm Miko's changeling."

Michiko stood blocking her way. "At least tell me that you're taking precautions, you know, against getting pregnant."

Suki cocked her head and smiled at Michiko and the dark

glint in her eye returned as she spoke. "Why would I do that?" Her voice seemed to split into two voices speaking in unison. "It's a wife's duty to bear a man strong healthy babies..." Suki's voice became that of another woman, older and more in charge. "Children who will grow to respect their father and not abandon him when he's older."

Michiko was not simply creeped out or uneasy – she was terrified by what was happening. She slowly gave up the doorway to Suki, or what Suki had become.

"They will never leave him. I will never leave him, I made him that solemn promise." She looked darkly at Michiko, "You won't be telling anyone about this, will you? I would be especially irritated if Ted were to find out. You know, Michiko, I am not a fun person when I'm betrayed." Then as quickly as it had come on it lifted like a curtain in a performance. "Well, gotta go now! Caio!" She said cheerily and walked out the door leaving behind a shaken Michiko.

Michiko sat in class behind Kuno and watched him from the back. She saw him gazing out the window at the girls in gym class – for which she would usually have given him a little jealous pinch – but today she just watched, as they seemed to elicit a bored yawn from him.

"I miss it." Kuno said, still half looking out the window and whispering to her.

Michiko was confused. "Miss what?"

"Your little pinch for eye-groping the freshman girls gym

class." He whispered, "Ever since the Fireworks Festival and with you at the Shrine I just can't get into other girls."

Michiko blushed but gave a little smile and reached out for his hand. "Yeah, that was… intense."

"Understatement? From you?"

Eager to change the subject she whispered into his ear. "Come with me outside where we can talk. It's about Suki."

"Okay." Confused, Kuno got up and followed Michiko out into the hall and down to a quiet stairwell.

"I'm worried about Suki." Michiko's eyes darted around to see if anyone could hear her. "Last night she changed."

"What do you mean 'changed'? Like she became moody?"

"I mean she took on an entirely different personality, a strange woman's personality, an older woman's voice and mannerisms. She became scary and… dangerous."

"Did she threaten you?"

"Not directly, it was more like a promise of payback if I stood in her way."

"Stood in the way of what?"

"Her and Ted."

"What would you have to do with Ted?"

"I know about her plan to take Ted's dead wife's place in his life. I think Miko may have turned the tables on Suki and taken her over instead."

Kuno was quiet for a moment and looked Michiko in the eye. "Do you understand how nuts that sounds?"

Michiko gave a frown. "Yeah, unfortunately, I do."

"Michiko, tell me, how much do you know about Suki?"

She stared at Kuno for a long moment. "That's a good question. I never thought much about it. We met in a class when we were freshmen and I needed a roommate, so I invited her to live in the dorm with me."

So, how much do you actually know about her? Like, when is her birthday?

"I asked her once but she never told me."

"What town is she from?"

Michiko gave Kuno a blank stare.

"What schools did she attend?"

"I-I don't know. She never told me."

"Does she talk about her family?"

"No. She always finds reason to change the subject. I think it upsets her."

"We need to learn more about sweet, innocent Suki. She's just become a mystery woman."

Friends and Illusions

"Michiko, Kuno! Wait up!" Miss Kusawa called from behind the couple as they walked down the hall.

Michiko turned to find Miss Kusawa jogging up behind them, her breasts bouncing and getting everyone's attention. Michiko said to Kuno "Miss K's so cute, she never changes."

"Yeah, she's cute." He discreetly took her hand in his and Michiko smiled. "But, you're cuter."

"So, you're over your fixation?"

"Which one? I have so many."

"With Miss Kusawa?"

"Her yes, you no."

"Guys I need to talk to you both about Suki. She missed the last two classes and when she did attend, she was disheveled and distracted and anxious about being in class, like she couldn't wait for it to end. What's happened to her?

Since the festival, she's been erratic and moody."

Michiko explained while hedging so Miss Kusawa wouldn't know Suki's real love. "She's been having some problems with her boyfriend."

"Oh no! He didn't dump her did he?"

"Just the opposite. All of our conniving and coaching paid off big time. He made a woman of her and now she's not just infatuated with him but obsessed. She took your advice and researched his ex-lover." Michiko wasn't lying. Dead, is as 'ex' as it gets. "Now she is trying to become her to please him. She spends a lot of time with him and comes to the dorm sometimes to sleep and then leaves in the morning to join him in his exercise and make breakfast for him . Then she does the marketing for him and cleans his room while he is out at breakfast every day. Then she works with him and they go out to coffee shops to talk about their shared academic interests."

"It sounds ideal." Miss Kusawa said as they walked along the halls towards her classroom.

"No, its scary!" Michiko was saddened by what Suki was going through. "She so wants to be the perfect model of the woman he loves, that she is losing herself to the other's personality." Michiko looked at Miss Kusawa and Kuno. "I think she's schizophrenic."

"Kind of a harsh diagnosis isn't it? What makes you think she's schizoid?" Miss Kusawa asked.

"She's falling deeper and deeper into this fantasy world of being her lover's wife… it won't end good." Michiko confessed. "She even spoke in the woman's voice. I heard it myself and confirmed it with a video she was able to find in her lover's home."

Kuno proposed, "Maybe she just wanted to make him feel more comfortable. You know, gradually wean him off his ex and onto her?"

"That's what she told me she was going to do: Kill his ex so all he would see only her."

"Kill her?" Miss Kusawa was shocked and concerned.

"Figuratively speaking, of course. She needs to kill his memories of her for him to see Suki and not Mi… the other woman. But I think she's letting the other possess her."

"Possessed?" Kuno laughed nervously. "You mean like exorcist stuff?"

"I don't know if it's spiritual or psychological, I only know that she's speaking in a voice that's not hers and the Suki we know is hiding underneath this new personality. At first I thought it was an act, but then I saw her change into the other woman – look like her; dress like her; wear her hair like her; walk like her and even sound like her - and it scared me shitless! It still does!"

Miss Kusawa offered. "More like a split personality."

"Yeah, something like that." Michiko became serious. "There's something else: The other night, I woke up and Suki was out on the balcony with her back against the railing. It was dark but she was looking into the room, staring at me. The light outside our building lit the top of her head but cast her face in shadows, yet I know she was intently looking at me. I asked her why she was out there in the cold with the door open. She began to move, crawling in my direction saying: 'Please don't get in my way. You are my friend and I don't want any misfortune to come to you. But Te… he is mine. And I love him forever.' She stood over me, staring wide-eyed at me with a maniacal look in her eyes. I can't describe it any other way. In the other woman's voice, she said they would spend eternity together. I don't think she was speaking romantically."

Miss Kusawa was somber as she listened to Michiko talk about Suki and she looked miserable. "We must help her, she's having a psychotic break. I think she meant what she said, and will do her boyfriend or anyone who comes between them – great harm."

For once, Kuno seemed to grasp the seriousness of the situation. "Do you mean she might hurt him?"

"Probably not, unless someone threatens her hold on him, like the other woman."

Michiko looked to her teacher with hopeless eyes. "So we have to find out who the woman is and warn her off, so not to agitate Suki?"

Miss Kusawa sighed. "How can we do that without alarming Suki? If you go to her boyfriend, he'll begin to act differently around her and that could spark paranoia in her, triggering a violent reaction."

Kuno said, "For an English teacher, you know a lot about psychology."

"Not really. This was all explained to me by the doctor who treated my mother."

"Your mother?"

"My mother had a psychotic break before… committing suicide."

"I'm sorry to hear that."

Miss Kusawa smiled weakly. "That was a long time ago."

Michiko realized that even though they'd known Miss Kusawa for two years, they knew so little about her. Now she was curious to know more, but thought she should change the subject.

"There's something else I need to talk to you about, woman-to-woman. It involves Suki and may be a bit, well, delicate." Michiko looked at Kuno.

"I get it, time for the guy to exit stage left before the girl talk begins." He walked over to Michiko and kissed her on the forehead.   "If you talk about me I'll know, because my ears will burn. See ya in the library." He waved to Miss Kusawa as he left. "See ya in class tomorrow Miss K."

She looked puzzled and turned to Michiko. "Miss K?"

"That's Kuno speak, he sees you as a good friend and feels its okay to give you a nickname."

"A friend? Really? That's nice. But I noticed that since the fireworks festival, he doesn't ogle me as much as he used to. I'm beginning to think that I'm becoming less desirable, or…" She turned a mischievous gaze Michiko's way. "…he finds a certain someone more desirable. " She looked at Michiko with a conspiratorial wink and a grin. "Confess, or I'll tear out your hair, one strand at a time until you talk!"

"Okay, but after school I need to have you to come back to the dorm with me."

Later, in the library, Kuno and Michiko looked up Suki's name in the university database.

"Isn't this confidential information?"

Kuno confirmed. "Yes, it is."

"Then how can you access it?"

"With the password."

"What I mean is, are you authorized to do this?"

Kuno looked at her and smiled. "Define 'authorized'."

Michiko looked at him. "Do I want to know how you got the password?"

"Do you want to be expelled if someone finds out?"

"No."

"Then you don't want to know."

"Fair enough." Michiko nodded "Start Digging."

Kuno found Suki's file without any problem. "Not the most flattering photo of her is it?"

"No, you're right. She looks entirely different now."

"Yeah, like someone else?"

"I was thinking that too."

Kuno scrolled down. "It lists her high school here. She tested high on the entrance exams. No surprise there since I copy her answers and pass every time."

Michiko punched him. "Lazy bum!"

"Ow! Not nice." Kuno peered at the file. "Hmmm."

"What did you find?"

"It shows her parents as deceased. She's an orphan."

"Maybe that's why she doesn't talk about her family."

"Her home address is in Mishima, but her emergency contact information is in care of a Miss Osuna Akani. It lists her title as Administrator of the Good Sheppard Home in Kannami.

"Can we print that?" Michiko asked Kuno.

"No, that's how they'll know there's been a breach. It shows up on their logs and they follow it up. Then they'll change the password and I have to start bribing people all over again. A screen shot doesn't register in their database."

"I knew there was something slightly felonious about you."

"You always liked bad boys!"

"Yeah, that's true." Michiko leaned down and gave him a peck on the cheek. "What else did you find?"

"Her birth date here is listed as 7 March. And her blood type is O positive."

"No, it's not. We went together to the campus blood drive last semester. The technician was happy she could donate since they don't get many A negative types."

Kuno peered at her. "Curiouser and curiouser."

"What about her address in Mishima? Can you look it up?"

"Yes, by using a local map directory, it's not a challenge." He moved through the pages of the directory and came to the address listed. "This is odd. It lists it as an inn."

"Maybe it's her family's business?"

"Maybe. The Proprietor's name is Mr. Honda."

"Kills that idea."

"Lets look up that home." After a minute the listing for the Good Sheppard Home came up. "It's a home run by the Catholic order, Sisters of the Sacred Heart. It's a home for…" Kuno stopped and let Michiko read the screen.

"Unwed mothers? What can that mean?"

"According to this, it's a sanctuary for unwed mothers to be cared for until their babies are born. Then they can decide to keep them or the sisters will take them in. It's a home and an orphanage." Kuno turned to Michiko. "Which one do you think Suki is, Mother or child?"

"Child. She's too naïve about men to be a mother. I can attest to Ted popping her at the festival, big time! Besides there's no evidence on her body of recent childbirth."

"So if it's an orphanage, and her parents are deceased this may be where she grew up."

Michiko shook her head. "So many things don't fit. The picture may resemble her a little if it's just a bad shot. Her blood type; the address in Mishima being a hotel; the name of the proprietor: It's all cockeyed."

Kuno proposed, "We need to take a road trip to Mishima and Kannami. They're only a hundred or so miles down the JR East line. We can be there in about two hours if we leave early."

"Maybe we can spend the night at the inn?"

Kuno volunteered. "I'll bring the ropes and handcuffs!"

"Great, and I'll use them on you so I can have a good night's sleep!"

The Shrine's Legacy

Opening the door to her dorm room, Michiko called out to Suki. No one answered. "Come on in. Suki's not home right now."

Miss Kusawa walked in and looked around. "It's been ages since I was in a dorm. Nothing's changed." She put her purse on the floor. "Can I use the bathroom? I had way too much tea today."

"Sure its back there to the right, hard to miss it in a small place like this."

After a moment Miss Kusawa came out with something in her hand. "Michiko is this yours?" She held out a package to show Michiko.

Michiko was in shock. "Pregnancy test strips? Not me, no way!"

"Then come with me." She led Michiko to the bathroom and showed her the spent strip in the wastebasket.

"What's it mean when it's blue like that?" Michiko asked

Miss Kusawa read the box. "According to this it means Suki's going to be a mommy."

"Holy crap! You've got to be kidding!"

She showed Michiko the box, which she read to make sure Miss Kusawa was not kidding.

"No wonder our napkin box is still full this month. She's been missing her period and now she pregnant with… his child." Michiko covered her mouth in horror. "What can we do?"

"Now its not just her but her baby that are in danger. If we threaten her; the baby; or the baby's father, she may become violent. So we have to be extremely cautious around her." Then she turned to Michiko. "With all the excitement, I almost forgot I went in to take a pee. BRB!"

Michiko started to think of ways she could reach out to her friend and roommate. Since finding out that Suki was possibly not whom she pretended to be, fear was the only emotion she could experience when Suki was around the dorm.

A minute later, Michiko heard a cry come from the bathroom. She ran to the locked door and pounded on it. "Miss Kusawa! Miss Kusawa! Are you all right?" Michiko heard the door unlatch, but not open. She slid the door back and saw Miss Kusawa with her back to her, facing the mirror, her reflection looked like she was in shock. "What happened?

"I just tried it for fun…" Miss Kusawa held up the blue strip in her shaking fingers. "I think… I'm pregnant!"

Michiko placed her arms around Miss Kusawa and walked her to the room and put out a chair for her to sit down. "Do you want some tea or juice or something?"

"This is a college dorm, don't you have anything stronger?"

"But if you're pregnant it wouldn't be good for the baby."

Miss Kusawa's lower lip quivered and she began bawling. "My baby's not even born and it's already changing my life!"

Michiko moved back to her side and tried to soothe her, placing her teacher's head against her belly and stroked her hair. "There, there, that's what little crumb snatchers do, they change your life."

"Pretty soon I'll be fat and all the boys won't find me sexy anymore, they'll laugh at me. And Takeshi, will he hate me for being so forgetful and not taking precautions?" Miss Kusawa sobbed.

"Shhh, he's a middle aged nerd who looks like a frog and had no romantic prospects until he met you. I think he'll be deliriously happy at the news."

"Careful that's my Mast… man your talking about." Her tone was defensive.

Michiko rubbed Miss Kusawa's shoulder vigorously. "That's the battle-bitch we all know and love!"

Miss Kusawa laughed and then sobbed again. But when I'm fat he won't find me attractive and we won't be able to do bond… er, that is..."

"Bondage? Oh, Mr. Suzuki seems to be a creative guy, I think he'll find a way to keep your S-M going."

"H-how did you know about us?"

"First there was the light reading materials in your drawer at school. If all the boys read only bondage and S-M magazines, that would be a VERY interesting class indeed." Michiko went on. "And then there was the fireworks festival. I told you that Kuno and I sealed the deal after his confession of love for me at the Fertility Shrine… but I didn't tell you where."

"So where did you two do it?"

"In the bushes… up at the playground."

"What a coincidence, Takeshi and I were up at the playground that night." She thought a moment. "Oh!"

"Eh, yeah, we were sort of following you two and saw you two from the bushes. Kuno suspected you were the Sub and Mr. Suzuki the Dom when he spotted the ropes beneath your robes. Which, may I say, really disappoints me since I always saw you as a dominatrix myself."

"Sorry."

"No. It's okay, because I was expecting to find a villain torturing a helpless female when we first hid. But as I watched him release you taking extra care not to harm you, and his saying all those sweet things to you, stroking your hair and then kissing you gently… It made me… real horny. Luckily Kuno was kneeling behind me, locked and loaded so I just backed into him and…"

"You and Kuno were there all the time?"

"Yes."

"And you were both watching me in bondage?"

"Yes."

"And it turned you both on?"

"Well, yeah, I guess… Definitely Kuno. I just knew he was doing me while watching and fantasizing about you. But that's okay because I want to indulge his fantasies to make him happy."

"Funny…"

"What's funny?"

"I remember hearing a muffled scream when leaving." She turned to Michiko. "Are you a screamer?"

Michiko was blushing bright red. "Yeah, I guess I am. People three blocks away know when I have an orgasm. That's why Kuno has me wear a gag when we have sex. I can't control myself."

"Gag? Sounds like you're on the road to becoming a Sub. Try having him tie your hands and putting a blindfold on you. It's beginner stuff but it really heightens the pleasure." Miss Kusawa was leaning her head into Michiko's womb as Michiko stood next to her, comforting her by stroking her hair.

"I'm not into that…" She paused. "Then again, watching you really did turn him on and it was the best sex I ever had, so I guess it couldn't hurt to suggest it to him.

"Michiko?"

"Yeah?"

"How long ago was the Fireworks Festival?"

"Almost two months, why"

"You mentioned that the napkin drawer is still full. That means that you didn't use any last month either?"

"Yeah, but I'm constantly missing my period. Doctor examined me when I was 16 and said I had a 50% chance of being sterile."

"That leaves a 50% chance that you're not sterile too."

"Yeah, but its crazy to think…"

"There's another strip in the bathroom."

"Are you suggesting that I might be…? Ha-ha, oh that's too funny."

"It's probably nothing, but I thought I heard something when I had my ear to your womb."

"Oh, that's just nuts."

"Bathroom's down and to the right."

"Okay, just to prove how crazy you are, I'll do it."

One minute later: "EEEEEEK!

Miss Kusawa pushed the door of the bathroom open. "Wow, you are a screamer!" She approached Michiko and stared at the blue strip in her hand. "That really is a powerful shrine!"

We're All Sisters Here

At dawn, Suki left Ted's compound, silently closing the gate bchind her to go back to her dorm for now and return to her classes. Ted felt she was neglecting her studies because of him. He was right, of course, they had been playing house for well over two months now, since the fireworks festival.

As Suki, she cooked and cleaned for him and worked by his side, but at night she gave herself to him as his late wife Miko, his lover. After so many years of living alone, he seemed to enjoy the attention. When he held her, he made her feel secure and wanted, even if he called her by another woman's name: it was *her* body he craved. For two weeks Ted neglected to make offerings at Miko's shrine: She had gotten him to quit mourning her. Suki was slowly killing Miko.

Walking up Osaka Road, away from Ted's gate, the small voice returned to whisper in her ear. 'We are happy? Sharing the man is good for now, but soon he will have to choose between us. You want him to see you, but I am the one who satisfies his desires, albeit through your body. I taught you the nuances that enchant him. From the yukata at the festival, to shaving, to the little nibble on his earlobe while making love, and letting him do "unusual" things to my body that excite him. How could you, a naïve country girl – a virgin – ever have known these things? You needed a teacher, and I obliged. The only payment I asked was to live again through you, and to love Ted forever, was it too much of you to give me that? Will you kill me and take my place?

'We will see which of us remains in the end.'

Miko was powerful. Suki wanted to argue with her but lacked the courage. Miko was greedy. When Suki undressed to make love to Ted, Miko drew back the covers and went to his side. She left Suki to become a spirit voyeur, hanging in the rafters like an insect, watching them embrace, jealously observing her seduce the man she loved.

Suki wanted her to share her body with Miko, but the avaricious entity left her with no memory of the many joys she should have rightfully experienced. Suki loved Ted, but Miko was siphoning all the joy out of being his lover. When they were spent and fulfilled, Miko left him to her. If he felt like a reprise late in the night or early morning, Miko returned and pushed her out of the conjugal bed. 'He is mine and I will have him forever!' Miko was fond of taunting her, saying she was no more than a vinyl doll for his desires and that only she gave him complete pleasure. Suki resented Miko, but took solace in having one thing that Miko could again never have with Ted: His baby.

Walking back to her dorm under the still burning

streetlamps, Suki rubbed her womb with contentment. The little voice startled her. 'That is his child too. Tell him and watch his reaction. He is old and has grownup children; do you think being a father again will make him happy? Will your baby please him or make him feel trapped?'

"Stop it!" Suki squatted against the wall and put her hands tightly over her ears to try to stop Miko's voice. "Leave our baby alone!"

'Oh, do you believe that is your baby? Ha-ha-ha… that is so precious! Who was he making love to at the festival? There was vitriol in her voice. ' The yukata, getas, the hair, the makeup, the voice, were they yours or mine? Did you seduce him or did I? Good little Suki, romantic, naïve Suki… you are no match for a woman with twenty-five years experience seducing Ted. You are just my conduit and the baby… well… let us see what becomes of it.' Miko's threat distressed her. Suki rose and began walking again. She had to escape Miko. Stepping up her pace she hoped to outrun the voice.

As she trotted in the dawn's pallid daylight, she looked around: Visions of the night she was attacked again surfaced. Running past the wall where the men pinned her and stripped her before Ted rescued her, she averted her eyes, as she had done every day since the incident. Darkness fell upon her and fear set in at times like these. 'You could not protect yourself. How can you hope to protect that baby?'

Breaking past the threshold of the dorm lobby in a cold sweat, she tried to recall how Ted carried her here and how he made her feel so safe. It calmed her and brought back a warm feeling of contentment inside. She placed her hands over her womb, and thought it was only right that the hero claim the fair damsel's chastity. She spoke to her unborn baby. "Ted is our hero, and we are his reward!"

The midwife at the lie-in clinic confirmed her pregnancy yesterday. The woman warned her that such a change in one's life is always a shock, and it creates confused thoughts before the acceptance sets in. Then she suggested an abortion. Killing her baby made her bristle and she angrily left the clinic. No one, in this world – or the next world – would come between her and her baby. Now all her thoughts were always about the baby and Ted and their happy sweet, sweet home together. Since discovering she would become a mother nothing else mattered.

Suki walked into her darkened room without turning on the lights, so not to wake Michiko. She would ask too many questions, which Suki would rather not answer right now. She quietly closed the door behind her.

"Suki?" Michiko's voice came from the balcony. When her eyes had adjusted, she saw a silhouette of Michiko sitting in her regular Ted watching seat.

"Ohio, Michiko-chan." There was a quiet, almost apologetic tone in her greeting, as she felt the guilt of ignoring her best friend.

Michiko was still for a moment. "Am I talking to Suki or..." Her voice came out in low, whispered caution. "...the other woman?"

She was taken aback by the curious way Michiko paused and phrased the question. "It's me, Suki."

"Then come and sit down." It was more of a parental command than a friend's request.

Suki put her bag down by the door and crossed the small room to where she usually sat with Michiko in the morning. As she came around the corner, someone else was sitting in her seat. "Sensei? Why are you here?"

"It's a long story." Miss Kusawa sighed. "Join us."

Suki took a stool from the room and sat between the two women.

Miss Kusawa leaned forward in her seat and looked curiously at Suki. "Are you all right?"

"Yes, I am well." It was the truth as best she knew it. "Thank you for asking."

She followed up her first question with another. "How is your boyfriend doing?"

"Very well, and happy." The line of questioning baffled Suki.

"And his ex? How has she been treating you?" Michiko asked with a slightly caustic tone to her voice.

Suki glared sharply at Michiko for bringing up the subject in front of Miss Kusawa. If she found out that her boyfriend was a gaijin, she would be angry. She detested them even though she herself was half one. "Please, don't..." She asked Michiko quietly. "She is quiet and I want her to stay that way."

"Does she come to you often?" asked Miss Kusawa.

Suki wasn't sure what to make of her teacher's question.

"Michiko told me about the problem you have with your boyfriends ex. I mean, how she takes over your personality. I understand better than you might think and I can help."

Suki turned a hateful gaze on Michiko. Her friend betrayed her. The glare wasn't Miko, Suki was furious. "Why did you tell her? I thought we were friends!" Suki fumed at Michiko.

The outburst startled Miss Kusawa, but didn't faze Michiko who just sat unperturbedly in her chair and stared Suki dead in the eyes. "Tell her." Michiko coldly commanded her roommate.

Suki was taken aback by Michiko's indifference towards her. She was Suki's only close friend and she wanted it to stay that way. She dropped her eyes and looked down to the floor.

Her confession came out soft and timid. "Sometimes, when I am about to make love to... my boyfriend. She takes over my body and when I wake up in the morning, I cannot remember our lovemaking. The only time I recall his being with me was the first time, when I let him take me at the festival. The fireworks burst as we climaxed and that is the last time I can remember experiencing any sensation, though we have been to bed many times." She became quiet. "He often asks me why I cry each morning. I tell him it is for joy, but it is not. It is because I am scared that I am insane."

Miss Kusawa took Suki's hand. "How did she come to

you?"

Suki looked into her gentle green eyes, which seemed so strange, yet familiar, and they made her feel comfortable. "While watching and re-watching the videos of her and looking at her photos for days without sleep, I absorbed her Ki. I tried so hard to imagine myself as her, that she came to me to guide me. Her spirit took over mine to teach me the ways of a woman." Suki bowed her head so her bangs covered her eyes, hiding them in shadows. "She pushes me out of my own body. No matter what I do, she is there, whispering in my ear, taunting me: She will not be happy until I am gone and she is reborn in my skin."

"Reborn?"

Michiko chimed in to save her friend. "It's just a turn of phrase she picked up from her English studies."

"Does your boyfriend know everything about you?" Miss Kusawa asked.

"No one knows everything about Suki." Michiko laughed. "Not even me. I don't know her birthday and we've lived together for almost two years." Michiko held a small strip of paper between her fingers. "Does he know about this?"

Suki looked up between the strands of hair falling over her eyes and saw the strip of paper fluttering in the breeze. The strip she ran from the other day when it so horrified her at first. It still made her stomach tighten and her breath shorten with anxiety. "No, he doesn't know about the baby."

'Oh look! They know you're dirty little secret!' Miko was

exuberant, her voice no longer quiet and suggestive, but loud as her own in her head. 'The dirty little love child is having her own love child! Ha-ha-ha, oh the irony, Suki, the irony! Its really very funny if you think about it.'

Suki gave a short snigger. Then she reared her head back and gave a loud laugh and laughed until tears ran down her cheeks. The two women were being treated to Miko's presence, looking into Miko's face. "Michiko, you so enjoy torturing poor Suki. You are so vicious for a 'friend'. I like that!"

"That voice…" Miss Kusawa stared at the girl, terrified. "That's not Suki's voice… I…!"

Suki looked at her askance, through matted hair, interrupting her. "And you, Ayako, aren't there dirty little secrets you've been hiding from everyone. It can't just be me."

"Stop it, Mi… Suki!" Michiko called to her. "This isn't your test strip! It's… mine." Michiko became silent.

Suki was shocked, and like a curtain lifting, Miko was gone and only Suki remained. "Y-yours? I don't understand. If it's yours and positive, that means that you're…" Suki stopped and placed her hands over her mouth so not to say the word.

"Pregnant." There was no joy in her voice as she let loose of the strip and it floated away on the breeze. "Yep, Kuno's gonna be a daddy. Whoopee."

"Have you told him?"

Miss Kusawa answered, "No. We only found out last

evening. We've been sitting up all night talking about what to do about it."

Suki looked at Michiko. "You love Kuno, and always have since you were both young, and I know he's crazy about you. What is there to consider? You are having his baby." There was finality in her statement.

"But what if he freaks out and doesn't want the baby?" Tears began to well in her eyes.

"I'll take care of him." Suki said to her. "He thinks I'm psycho and if I threaten to cut his balls off if he doesn't marry you, he'll think I'm serious." Suki gave her innocent smile as she said it.

Michiko looked at her as if she was serious, and then began to laugh through her tears. "You would, wouldn't you? That might work with Kuno, but not Mr. Suzuki."

"Why Mr. Suzuki? She looked at Miss Kusawa who was trying to wave off Michiko.

"Oh go ahead and show her, we're all sisters here." Michiko said.

Miss Kusawa sighed and produced her positive test strip.

Suki's eyes grew large. "You too, Miss Kusawa? You're going to have a baby too?"

Miss Kusawa muttered, "Damn that shrine!"

"Yeah." Michiko seconded it. "I'm never going back there. And remind me to beat that doctor who said I should be sterile." Then her frown turned into a soft, contented smile. "Which, it turns out, I'm not."

Suki reached out and hugged Miss Kusawa and waved for Michiko to join them. Together they cried and laughed and now shared a bond that would tie them together forever. As the little voice tried to interrupt, Suki just hugged the other women tighter until she went away.

Finding Suki

Getting out of the cab Michiko looked up at the Pink Patio Inn as Kuno paid the driver.

Kuno stood next to her carrying their luggage. "So, what do you think?"

"I think this where our search for Suki begins."

Walking into the inn they saw the small restaurant in the lobby and decided to have some tea and sweets after their trip. Sitting by the window, Michiko looked out over the town, down the hill from the inn. The Hakano Mountains in the distance and the Kano River meandering through the town. "It's different from the city. Things seem to move slower here." She pulled a folder from her backpack and put it on the table.

Kuno reached for it and opened it. "Including the service." His snide comment just missed the ears of the waitress as she approached.

"Hello, welcome to the Pink Patio, how can I help you

today?" The cheery voice said. "Today's special is the Seafood Udon. "She handed the menus to Michiko and Kuno.

He took it without looking up and perused it quickly. "I'll have the house tea and some cake." He handed the menu back without looking and turned his attention back to the file of research material they had on Suki.

Michiko handed the menu back. "The Udon sounds great. I'll have that and the iced tea..." She read the waitresses nametag. "...Suki, thanks."

Kuno had his head buried in the folder. "You've been eating a lot lately. Better be careful or you'll get fat."

Michiko angrily snapped apart the chopsticks. "Never call a woman fat! Full figured, Rubenesque, pleasantly plump... anything but fat!"

"Two-tons of fun?"

"No! That's worse!"

"I was talking about your jugs. They're gotten bigger, rounder, firmer, so fully packed!"

Michiko looked down at her cleavage, which was pushed together. "You think so?"

"My hands never lie." Kuno said. "What was that about Suki?"

"Huh?"

"I wasn't listening closely. You mentioned Suki."

Michiko thought for a moment. "Oh, I was just giving my

order to the waitress. Her name is Suki. Father always said that you get the best service if you smile and call you waitress by her name."

"Kuno shrugged. "Must be a common name in these parts."

"So what do we do first? We can go to the prefecture records to look her up." Michiko said.

"No that would take the better part of the day. I'm for going to the orphanage first and asking questions there."

"Yeah, but they're so far apart. The taxi fare will break our budget."

Kuno handed her the scan of the university student's information sheet they got from the Internet. "This is one of the addresses given, maybe we can start here?"

Michiko looked at him. "I thought you said this was just a bogus address that she put down."

"Now that we're here, I'm not so sure."

The waitress returned with Kuno's tea and cake and Michiko's iced tea. "The Udon will be ready in a few minutes."

Michiko looked up at the waitress and then down at the student record. "Eh, thanks." When the waitress left she pushed the file in front of Kuno. She whispered, "Look at this!" She was pointing to the picture of Suki in the file."

"Uh, okay. I'm looking at it. So?"

"Look at our waitress."

Kuno looked up at the waitress talking to the proprietor of the inn.

Michiko said, "Looks kinda like her, doesn't it?"

He looked back to the photo and then at the waitress. "Yeah, it really does."

"We have to find out more about this. It's just too much of a coincidence. What do we do now?" Michiko asked.

"Here she comes with the udon. I suggest we eat."

During the meal they discussed what they should do. Kuno finally asked her, "Did you bring the wedding bands as I suggested?"

"Yeah, I got these from a friend at the dorm."

"What does she use them for?"

"So she could go out with friends and not get hit on by guys."

"But lots of guys get off on married women."

"Yeah, she found that out too."

"Well let's put them on and flash them at the waitress when she comes with the bill."

When the waitress returned, Kuno talked to her. "Excuse me, my wife and I are newlyweds travelling through the area. Do you have a room we can rent?"

"We certainly do. When you are finished, I can show you around some of the rooms, including our honeymoon suite." She smiled.

Michiko was taken aback. "Honey…?"

Kuno interrupted Michiko. "Yes, Dear, I love you too." He turned to the waitress. "Thank you for you kindness, that will be fine."

When the waitress left with their payment, Michiko leaned over and whispered through clenched teeth. "Aren't we taking this newlywed ploy a little to seriously? I mean, the honeymoon suite!"

"We need to get her alone to talk to her. I think she's key to our finding out about Suki… or whoever she is,"

"How can you say that? Suki's been our friend for over two years."

"I don't doubt that she's our friend. I just have doubts that she's who she says she is."

On the way to the rooms they walked along a railing that overlooked the town.

Michiko looked out over the hamlet. "This is quite a nice town. Peaceful and quiet." She turned to their guide. "Have you lived in Mishima all your life?"

Suki, the waitress, answered Michiko with a smile. "No. I'm originally from Kannami, across the hill. I came here to live with my uncle, after my aunt died. He lets me stay here with my son for free."

"You have a son?"

"Yes, he's a two years old. His name is Kei."

"How surprising. You don't look that old yourself."

"I'm actually twenty. I was scheduled to go to the university, but having Kei changed my priorities."

"Oh, I'm sorry." Michiko said.

"Don't be. Having a child is wonderful. It completes me as a woman." She smiled and then a hint of sadness crossed her face. "I'm almost glad that girl stole my things."

Kuno asked her. "A girl stole your things?"

"Yes, when I went to the home to have Kei, I had planned to put him up for adoption and continue on to the university. A girl I met there, an orphan about to be turned out, befriended me and then stole my bag with my transcripts, it changed everything."

Michiko asked, "Home?"

"Yes, Good Sheppard, over the hill."

Michiko asked her, "Suki, what is your family name?"

"It is Ona. Ona Suki."

"When I held Kei, I knew I could never give him up so I decided to abandon going to college. My uncle, who is my mother's younger brother, was kind enough to give me a home and job. Someday he said I'll inherit this inn from him, so Kei and I never have to worry."

"You said the girl that stole your things was about to be turned out. What does that mean?"

"The home is there to help young unwed mothers… like me. If a mother leaves her child, the sisters try to find a family for the baby. Sometimes children don't get adopted right away but the older they get the more difficult it is to place them. Junko was never adopted. At age seventeen, she had to leave the orphanage.

Michiko frowned. "That's so cruel."

"When I made friends with her, the Administrator pulled me aside and told me to avoid her, that she was troublesome and mentally unstable."

"Was she?" Kuno asked.

"Kuno! That's not nice to ask!" Michiko turned from Kuno to Suki. "Was she?"

"She was a little bit strange. In the months I was there I got to know her and she seemed fine, but I also heard gossip from the staff."

"Like what?"

"They said things like: she was the love child of a young teenager who had an incestuous affaire; That Junko was not right in the head; She obsessed about who her father was, but no one would tell her. There was rumor that her mother came by once a year on her birthday to visit, but stopped about six years before. She never returned. Someone said she married and kept Junko a secret from her husband.

"What was Junko like?"

"Junko was very shy and timid. The staff treated her like a servant. They physically and emotionally abused her but she still smiled and was kind to others. She wanted to please everyone."

Kuno snorted. "That may be what made her crazy!"

"She was smart and wanted to go to college, but the Chief Administrator disliked her and refused to sponsor her to a school. That meant going to a trade school where she could learn secretarial or office skills… or the streets as a bargirl. She said she wanted to go to school to make her mother proud and to find her father so they could be a family." Suki waned sad. "She said birthing a child was the most important thing a woman can do. We talked about the baby and in time she convinced me to keep the baby and give up going to the university. Soon after, she disappeared with my bag. Inside were my transcripts and acceptance letter with my identification."

Michiko took out a photo of her, Kuno and Suki and showed to it the girl. "Is this Junko?"

The girl barely glanced at the photo before turning away. "That's her." Her voice was small and neutral. Suki turned away facing the town beyond the railing and was quiet for a long moment before asking, "How is she?"

Michiko had expected something akin to outrage or anger, but was surprised by with girl's concern for the one who took away her future.

"She's an honor student, but seems to be having some... well, issues. She's gotten involved with an older man and is taking on another personality. Were here because we're worried about her."

Suki just nodded and sighed.

"You don't seem surprised."

"The way she was treated all her life? No, I'm only surprised she's done as well as she has. You do know that the older man is the father she never knew." She was silent for a moment. "Tell me about the personality you mentioned."

Michiko was perplexed by this girl's sympathetic attitude to the one who stole her identity. "The personality is the dead wife of the man she loves. She takes on Miko's personality and traits when she makes love to her boyfriend.

"Miko?" For the first time, Suki's eyes were alert here brow wrinkled and she focused here eyes on Michiko. "The woman's name is Miko?"

"Yeah, that was his late wife's name." Kuno said.

"Suki shook her head. "Poor Junko!"

"What's the matter?" Michiko asked.

Suki's eyes became moist. "Miko was Junko's mother."

A Hopeful Truce

Suki had been able to keep Miko at bay for a week. With Ted, she was able to control her passions so not to give Miko an opening to enter and pervert their love. She was more businesslike around Ted without putting him off, only cooling the sexual passion for a more loving day-to-day happiness. She would touch and casually kiss him to assure her interest, but returned to the 'Suki look' and tried to get him to see her instead of Miko. She knew that Miko was waiting for an opening to take over. Though she desperately wanted to love him, she contained her passions in order to keep him to herself. Miko was quiet and she wanted to keep it that way.

It was Friday and she decided to go to the market before reporting to work. She thought it would be nice if she were to make him okinomiyaki and tempura udon for dinner. Shopping for him with his baby inside made her very happy. She was the good wife and mother.

Mother. Rather than the warm emotion she wanted to feel, the word gave her a chill.

A cry resonated from a dark place, but it wasn't Miko's

voice. This tiny panicked voice was a child calling out her mother's name and reaching out, only for others pulled her away. She felt the separation. Many voices said 'an evil mother'; 'too young to be a mother'; 'what kind of mother would do that to her child?'

Suki became dizzy and her knees began to buckle as she searched out someplace to sit down. She found a bench in the food court. Her head was spinning with the fragments of her past. Miko's voice came to comfort her. 'Dear Suki, I know how it feels to be called a bad mother. My own people persecuted me for marrying outside my race. Isolated me. Drove me closer to Ted. He was all I had.'

"I'm sorry Miko." Suki spoke to the voice that haunted her. "I know it was hard for you. But you came from a prominent family and the rejection was hard. You lost family, friends, prestige for the love of Ted." She was quiet for a moment, as she had reached a peaceful accord with the voice in her head. Then her continence changed and a dark veil fell over her. "That is why you have returned to him through me; you seek retribution for your pain. You want him to suffer as you suffered. You want him dead, so he will be with you." She began to cry. "You can't have him! I'LL DIE FIRST!"

Her outburst brought embarrassing attention and she looked around at all the surprised faces staring at her. One, an elderly fishmonger from one of the stalls, came to her and placed her hand on her shoulder.

"Are you all right, dear?" She looked at Suki with smiling, wrinkled eyes. "It seems that you are a little pale and drawn. Can I get you some tea to help calm your nerves?"

Suki just wanted to run away. Her weak knees had not recovered and she was shaking. The old woman's offer seemed enticing. "That would be very kind of you. I guess I didn't realize how weak I am."

A short moment later she returned with the tea and placed the cup before Suki.

She gave the venerable woman an apology. "I am sorry for my outburst. Please forgive me."

The old woman looked at her, puzzled. "Why do you seek forgiveness?"

"My thoughts are confused, my emotions are tender and easily provoked. It is shameful behavior."

"Not at all dear, it is most natural for an expectant mother to be sensitive in her emotions. When is your baby due?"

She was shocked and looked to her belly, which was not yet protruding. She looked at the old woman's smile. "H-how did you guess? I'm not showing yet." Then she put her hand over her mouth having blurted out a secret she kept to herself.

"Look at this face. It has seen five daughters and three granddaughters marry and have children. With luck I may live long enough to see a great granddaughter have hers too." She leaned over and winked at Suki. "I am very ancient!"

"No you are the face of acquired happiness. It is beautiful."

"So young and so very gracious!" The old woman giggled. "But child, do not fret if your emotions are causing you concern, it is natural. You body is changing, preparing you for motherhood. To be a good mother."

"But what mother would a bring a curse on her child before it is even born?"

"What do you mean dear?"

"My baby's father is… gaijin."

The old woman felt Suki's sadness and confusion but didn't seem to be put off or shocked. She just sighed. "As I have told you, I had five daughters of eight children. My second daughter fell in love with a Gaikokujin from Europe. Rather than shame our family she went to live with him and his family. They took her in as one of their own and accepted her. It is something she would not have here where she would be outside of society." The old woman looked cheerless. "In the end the shame was mine. I did not watch my grandchildren grow up into fine adults. One year they visited Japan and came to see me, for my husband was long dead and my daughter would no longer have to face his disapproval. She expected me to turn her and her children away. I had practiced words in their language for the day I would meet them. I said, 'welcome to your grandmother's home, where you are loved.' It was all I knew to say to them. They responded by running to hug me. It was all I needed to know and all they needed to hear."

Suki was shedding a tear at the old woman's story.

"I brought my daughter and grandchildren here to

introduce them to all my friends and to show how proud I was of them. It was then that I found my true friends and weeded out the false ones. A true friend will always want to share in your happiness, while a false one judges you by what they can get from you."

"What of my child will he or she have to endure rejection by people if we remain here?"

The old woman took Suki's hand. "If you go into such a marriage expecting rejection that is what you will get. Expect acceptance and you will have it. With the love of a good husband neither will matter."

"What is your name, grandmother?"

"I am called Nana."

Suki rose and gave a great and deep bow to the woman. "Your tea has calmed my nerves and your words have calmed my soul. Domo Arigato, Nana-sama." She picked up her bags and prepared to leave. "I hope we will meet again."

"And so do I child. You must take good care of yourself. Goodbye."

Unraveling Suki

Kuno and Michiko stood before a house in a middle class neighborhood of Mishima. It did not stand out among the others that surrounded it. There were a few individual affections outside and it was a study in social conformity and blandness: Fitting in, so not to stand out. It was as if Junko's mother wanted to disappear into the background of polite society. She had found the perfect place to hide from her sins.

The waitress – the real Suki – gave them this address. For some time she had tried to track Junko down to retrieve her things, eventually giving up and accepting the life she had been given as her fate.

Knocking on the door they half expected a monster to come out and devour them. Instead, a young boy cracked the door open and peeked out. They looked down. "Hi, is your mother, Miko, here?" Michiko asked. The little boy just shook his head and shut the door. They heard his feet scampering away. They looked at one another and turned to walk back down the stairs.

"It's hard to argue with a little gatekeeper like that." Kuno said.

As they reached the gate and prepared to leave, a frail, old voice called out to them. "Were you her friends?"

Because of the age difference, they came up with a plausible excuse for calling on Junko's mother. Kuno called back. "No, my mother knew her from many years back, when our family lived here. She asked us to drop by and pay our respects."

She invited the couple inside.

Kuno and Michiko sat up straight as the old woman poured them tea. "Would you like a biscuit to go with that?"

Michiko declined the offer. "Oh, no thank you. We just ate."

"It's nice that you came all this way to pay your respects. Young people these days seldom display such manners.

"My mother said they played together as children. When I told her we were spending our honeymoon here, she asked me to look her up and say hello." Kuno looked up at the picture of Junko's mother and whispered to Michiko, "She looks exactly like Suki."

The old woman's ears perked up as she sipped her tea. "Who is Suki?"

Michiko tried to cover for Kuno. "Oh, just my roommate at the university."

The old woman calmly eyed Michiko. "What is your age,

about 19 or 20?"

"Yes, I'm 19." Michiko said.

"Do you have a picture of your friend?"

Michiko began tripping over herself to backtrack. "Oh, well you see, I…" She felt Kuno's hand on her arm.

Looking at her, he nodded. "Go ahead. Show it to her. It's the least we can do."

Michiko reached into her purse bringing out the snapshot of them and handed it to the old woman.

"I knew that your mother didn't grow up here with her. Miko moved in with me when she was fourteen – after she already had her baby. I was just puzzled and needed to know why you really came here. Call it an old woman's curiosity."   She looked at the photo for a long time. "You're right… She's a few years younger, but she could have been her twin sister." She looked up at the picture of Junko's mother on the shelf sitting behind burnt incense, the food offering and the urn holding Miko's ashes.

After dropping the boy off with her neighbor, the old woman walked down the stairs to meet them. "Let's take a walk and I'll tell you everything."   The three of them headed down the street towards the river.

Kuno offered his condolences   "We're sorry about your daughter's death."

"She wasn't my daughter." The old woman said walking along holding her hands behind her back and her head inclined down towards the pavement. "She was my niece."

Without looking up she explained. When she became pregnant at age 13 her mother, my sister-in-law, needed to cover up the scandal and sent her to that home. She used the excuse that her daughter had received a scholarship to a prep school and had to leave immediately.

 "Her older half brother, from a previous marriage, raped her with the help of some of his friends." The old woman spat. " After the baby was born and left with the Sisters, my brother pleaded with me to take Miko in to preserve his reputation in the community. So I hid her here, far away from them, on the condition they were never to contact her again.

 "She went to school here and seemed to be doing fine. Every year on the child's birthday she would visit her with a small present. She was waiting for the time when she was old enough to retrieve her, until she fell for a local boy who she called her Prince Charming. Well he was charming and all the girls at her school knew intimately about his charms. Yet for some inexplicable reason he married her. She was a bit of a dreamer and talked about her sweet, sweet home and her happy life with him." She snorted and stopped at the curb. Looking right and left, she crossed the street to the levee that sloped down to the river below. She turned left towards the bridge that spanned the waterway. "She seemed very happy at first. They had a son, Hiro – you met him at the house: a nice boy, but a bit shy – who would be your Suki's half brother."

 She walked out to the center of the bridge and looked down the river towards the harbor in the distance. "Waters here look still but below they are turbulent and deceptively swift." She gazed out to the distant harbor. "A few years into the marriage, he became discontent with her and took a mistress, Miko's best friend. She let him beat her and was even willing to overlook the other woman for her happy ending." The old woman dropped a piece of paper, a prayer, into the waters and watched it float away. "On the day he asked her for a divorce. We found her shoes here. No note or anything else. Three days later her body was found washed up on the shore across the bay."

Yes, Mommy

Suki felt very happy on her walk back to Ted's house from the market. The old woman's kind words had given her comfort and the courage to endure. She determined to focus only on her family: Ted and their baby, nothing else mattered.

Suki felt a presence nearby. She knew something was there: an inaudible sense of someone overtaking her on a lonely road. Not knowing the other's motives, she feared the worst. Since the attack, she was more aware of her surroundings. She gave a short, furtive gaze over her shoulder to see who was there. Suki saw nothing and heaved a relaxed sigh. Something moved at the fringe of her vision. The ominous sensation returned with an electric charge, making her arm hairs stand erect, pulling the flesh up with them, rippling in waves and bumps. Her spine straightened. She kept her eyes forward, waiting. When she cautiously turned her eyes she saw nothing. Again, looking ahead, it reappeared as an indistinct image, floating just outside of her ability to truly see it: it appeared to be a woman.   The wraithlike apparition moved out of her peripheral vision and took on a yellowed tint. Suki saw her as if she had walked out of an old home movie. The ethereal woman's dress looked familiar to Suki.

"Why do you follow me?" Suki asked the chimera, hoping not to receive an answer.

'Where else can I go? We are one soul', the tiny voice in Suki's head took on a new resonance, as loud as someone standing next to her, talking.

"You are an Oni, you should go to hell." Suki quickened her steps, avoiding eye contact with the demon.

'Oh Suki, you hurt my feelings. I have been to hell. I prefer not to go back, at least, not alone.'

"You can't have Ted, Miko. He is alive for the first time in years. He has stopped dying, he has stopped mourning you."

'It is true that I was displeased about dying, but his sacrifices appeased my soul so I could endure it. When he forgot about me, only then did I truly begin dying. I decided to come and see why he forsook me. That is when I first saw you from my memorial. You were the reason he was forgetting me. So, I led you to the photos and videos. Once you saw me as Ted did I could enter into you and again touch my lover with your hands. For that, I should thank you, but you are stubborn and will not surrender yourself to me. You want Ted all to yourself. I cannot allow that.'

Suki turned to challenge the specter, but Miko just slipped

away beyond the borders of her vision. Suki's spirit rival became more of a notion than an image.

Twisting her head forward again, Suki clutched at her grocery sack as she picked up her pace towards the sanctuary of Ted's home. "You are nothing but a tiny voice in my head, a bit of a distraction. That is all. I can ignore you."

'Oh? You can ignore me? Then why aren't you?' The voice taunted her. 'I see, you think that I am not real, that I am only a illusion your imagination has concocted.'

"Yes. A good doctor and a bit of medication will make you go away."

Suki rushed along hoping to ignore Miko's taunts, but something caught her arm and whipped her around, causing her to drop her grocery bag. She found herself staring directly into Miko's face: just as she saw her in the videos.

"Take a good look, you little bitch! Are these the eyes of a ghost staring at you? Is this the sound of a spirit? And are these..." Miko's specter reached out, took Suki's cheeks into her clammy hands, and moved the petrified girl's face up to her own. "...the touch and kiss..." She pressed warm lips to Suki's. "...of a corpse?" Miko's red lipstick was tacky on Suki's lips: her breath, putrefied with a charred odor.

Suki recoiled, first blinking rapidly and then shutting her eyes tight. When she opened them, the visage was gone and all was hushed, like someone had switched off a television. She looked at her sleeve, which had caught on a nail protruding from the lamppost. She shuddered, feeling violated. Releasing her sleeve and picking up her spilled groceries, she ran in a panic towards Ted's home.

 Once through the gate her heart calmed a bit and she could relax. This courtyard was a familiar place, a safe place. Walking up to the hall leading towards Ted's room, she removed her street shoes. Looking down Suki saw a pair of women's shoes. They were not hers; they were too large. She heard a woman's voice coming from Ted's room. Moving into the hall and hiding behind a wooden post, Suki strained to hear beyond the thin, closed door as it slid open. Suki moved around the corner and pressed herself flat against the wall so not to be discovered. Ted passed by her with another woman. He had his arm around her shoulder as they walked towards the gate. They talked softly and intimately between one another – as she and Ted often did so not to wake the neighbors. Were they whispers of clandestine love or simply small talk? Suki could not hear their conversation. His arm around her showed his affection and she accepted his embrace comfortably. They had embraced this way before. Her rival's black hair hung loose and obscured the woman's face from view. Her voice was only a suggestion, like that of an autumn breeze whispering through the trees.

'Oh, look! The other woman you saw from your balcony. She's quite tall isn't she? How tall are you Suki? 158, 160 centimeters?' Miko squatted on her haunches in the shadow of Suki's vision, deep within recesses of a dark corridor. 'She must be at least 175 centimeters. I myself was 170. Ted likes his women tall.' Miko's voice foamed with contempt.

As the woman prepared to leave, she gave Ted a quick, friendly buff on his cheek, which brought a smile to his face.

'How sweet. She seems to bring out the best in him.'

Ted closed the gate and walked back to his room passing the area where Suki had hidden.   Now empty, Suki retreated into the darkness of the unlit hallway, to where Miko squatted, opposite of the hall leading to Ted's room. Numb from the shock of the other woman kissing her man, Suki listened to the small watery voice coming from behind her, whispering in her ear as she felt the embrace of ghostly arms encasing her shoulders and breasts. 'Welcome to the shadows Suki.'

Suki gave no reply to Miko taunts and enticements. Numbness from the cold stab of betrayal left her without the will to resist and she gave way to the oni's stark embrace and her soothing voice. 'Your mother abandoned you after your father impregnated her. She sent you to live among strangers. Everyone hates a love child. But Suki, I can be your good mother.' Miko comforted her. 'You need my embrace and my affection and I will stroke your hair and tell you how beautiful you are.'   Suki felt the constricting bonds of Miko's embrace tensing around her chest, like ropes being pulled taut, as the ghost gently whispered in her ear, 'Call me, Mommy.'

Tears trickled down Suki's cheeks and she let loose, no longer able to hold back. She bowed her head, letting the torrent of her sorrows pour forth. She reared her head back and whimpered, "Mommy!" In that moment she became happy, warm and contented. She was now the child of

Miko, her Mommy. She felt the comfort of a mother's love clotting to choke the tears out of her. She reached up to take hold of the arms that held her but were not there.

'Shhh, be still now; you are a good girl. I am here for you. Be happy.' Suki felt Miko's dead hand stroking her hair. 'Mommy loves you.'

Suki longed to hear those word all of her life: Words her mother never spoke to her; Words teachers at the home would not say to her. All anyone offered her was mortification and scorn. Stories told to her by cruel teachers and others were that she was a 'child of incestuous rape and thrown away, as a used condom is flushed down a toilet.' -- Even allowing dissolute older boys to use her as their toilet. She was effluent, the cast off of a carnal lust her uncle held for her barely pubescent mother. Suki sought love, but lived in terror and lament. Against the odds, she preserved her virginity all those years to give it to Ted, the only man she ever loved. When she received her scholarship to the university she vowed to never let anyone humiliate her again.

'He got what he wanted from you and threw your love back in your face, didn't he, my precious little girl?' Suki listened to Miko, whose tone transformed from pity to anger. The ghost hissed in her ear, 'He needs to be punished.'

"How Mommy? How can I hurt him?" Suki asked: her voice vacant and eyes glazed.

'Take away all that that he holds dear.'

"The woman?"

'Yes! Remove her and you send him into the living hell of endless regret and timeless pain.'

"Like he felt for you when you died Mommy?"

Miko's voice went silent for a moment. Suki heard a barely audible, 'Yes.'

Suki stood up. "I'll take her away from him." She walked out of the dark corridor into the stormy afternoon daylight.

'Wait!' The voice whispered in one ear and then the other. 'The knife, take it!'

Suki looked down into the grocery bag and saw the handle of a kitchen knife she had bought in the market that morning. Miko slid the bag across to her, offering the knife. Suki reached down and took the handle of the new knife as it reflected severe red-rimmed eyes in its shiny blade. She looked back at Miko's face smiling up at her, charming and colorless. Suki smiled back, saying, "Thank you Mommy."

'What else is a mother for, if not to help her baby?'

Suki closed the gate and watched the woman disappear around the corner. She slipped the knife up her blouse sleeve, the one with the tear left by a nail when Miko swung her around. Carrying a knife might give people the idea that she was crazy or something. She was not crazy. She was sane. She was a good girl. Mother said so. Mothers never lie.

As she stalked her prey down the road, Suki felt the first drops of rain fall in her eyes. Soon, the rain became a storm. She did not feel wet. Suki walked around the corner and saw that the woman had drawn her umbrella. A flash of lightning and the crack of thunder startled the woman. The storm was a blessing to Suki: It would let her to sneak up on the woman and put the knife into her belly – the thunder would absorb her screams and rain would wash away her blood. Visions of the woman's diluted blood running down storm drains made Suki lick her wet lips and grin. She was now impatient for the kill: but first, the joy of the hunt.

She followed the woman up a short hill, the same route she and Michiko often took to school. Suki knew every opportune spot along this street to ambush the woman. She got within five meters of her prey when the woman stumbled. Suki hid behind a telephone post as she watched the woman check her heel and then as she hobbled under an awning to check out her broken shoe. She placed the umbrella down and Suki should have gotten a good view of the woman's face, but with the rain obscuring her vision, it took a flash of lightening to expose her rival's identity.

Suki thought that maybe the rain in her eyes was causing them to play tricks on her. She wiped the wetness from her eyes, but not before the flash had passed. Soon there was another. This time there was no denying the identity of the other woman. The shock stabbed at her heart.

'Isn't that always the case?' Miko stood across from Suki leaning against a post box with her arms folded

Suki worried someone might see her, but remembered that Miko haunted only her. She stood there in her flowery summer dress with a hair band separating her bangs from the raised hair that tied up at the back of her head.

'It's always the one you trust the most who ends up betraying you.' Miko clicked her tongue and shook her head, with her arms crossed. 'Tsk, tsk. She's nice to your face and then when you're back's turned she's bedding down your husband.' Miko turned to Suki and smiled kindly. 'I know you like her sweetie, but she has to die.'

"Miss Kusawa?" Suki said, "It can't be her. She's my friend, my teacher. She helped me to learn how to seduce Ted." Suki turned apologetically to the ghost with a slight bow, "No offense."

'None taken. Actually, you were quite impressive with your ingenuity and dedication to getting him to bed you down. You may be my worthy successor after all.'

"Miss Kusawa hates gaijins, even though she's half white herself. She doesn't socialize with them." Miss Kusawa was moving again and Suki jogged to keep up with her. As she crested the hill, she saw Miss Kusawa walking towards the quad. There were too many people there for her to strike. She would have to follow her and wait for the right opportunity.

'Well she's pretty damn sociable with at least one gaijin!' Miko stayed with her talking to her as she stalked Miss Kusawa. 'It's funny he never mentioned her to you.' Suki looked over at Miko, still dry and wearing that summer dress, as she floated at her side. 'I'll bet he never mentioned you to her either. It's a guy thing.'

"Bitter old Oni!" Suki muttered, angry at her implication of Ted's duplicity.

'You shouldn't talk to your mother like that sweetie.' The

sweet, sunny countenance of Miko's face gave way to darkening around her eyes as they sank into the sockets of her skull. Then through a wide sardonic grin, she hissed. 'It just pisses the hell out of mommy!' Then the sweet face Suki saw in the videos returned. 'We shouldn't fight, sweetheart, we should join together to get this bitch who is taking away our man.' With that, the ghost of Miko entered Suki's body.

Miko possessing her soul made Suki dizzy. She steadied herself, looked around and saw all the other students staring at her, but why wouldn't they: It was pouring down rain and she strolled through the quad without an umbrella clutching at her arm. The women – Miko and Suki – regarded the students with contempt. What did they understand of her betrayal by a close friend and her lover? All she could do was keep her focus following Miss Kusawa, who stepped up her pace. She was probably late for her class again. If Suki wanted to get her, it would have to be before she reached her classroom. The elevator was always crowded at that time of day and it would certainly delay Miss Kusawa. Suki ran up the stairs at the end of the building to head her off. She hid inside the doorway of an empty, darkened classroom, waiting for Miss Kusawa to get off the elevator. Stroking the knife concealed underneath her sleeve gave her tender reassurance.

Miko was in complete control of Suki. 'Now, we finish it.'

Miko's will had become Suki's will. "Yes, Mommy."

The Other Woman

Suki had run up the stairs at the end of the building and made here way to the empty classroom nearest the elevator. Still wet from her stalking Miss Kusawa, her clothes clung to her petite body. There she waited for Miss Kusawa to come past the classroom where she could lure her in. Then she would unleash Miko on her rival.

"Miss Kusawa! What happened to you?"

It was Michiko's voice coming from the direction of the elevator. Suki peeked out of the doorway to see what was happening. 'That meddlesome girl will ruin your plans.' "No she won't.   I'll take care of everything." Suki whispered.

Miss Kusawa was tying her hair up as she answered Michiko, "Yeah, I was caught in a downpour with this cheap umbrella. That's the last time I'll get one from the sale table."

As Michiko and Miss Kusawa passed by the doorway of the empty classroom, Suki stepped out and approached them. "Miss Kusawa, do you have a moment? I have to speak with you."

"Suki, you're soaking wet." Miss Kusawa said. "That's can't be good for..." She whispered to her. "...Your baby."

Suki briefly made eye contact with Michiko, who seemed to know that she was looking at Miko and responded with a gaze of cold and suspicion. Suki, quickly averted her dark gaze and turned back to Miss Kusawa.

"You should be careful with your baby as well." Suki reminded her with a disarming smile. "Don't you keep a change of clothes in your coat closet in the classroom?

Miss Kusawa raised here fingers to her lips. "Shhh! The baby's still a state secret."

"Maybe Michiko can go and get them for you while we speak? I'll be done with you before she gets back."

"Yes, that's a good idea. Michiko can you please get the blue dress and white blouse for me? I'll change in the teachers restroom after I talk to Suki."

Okay, Miss K. I'll be back in a minute." Michiko said.

Suki gestured to the empty classroom. "Its private so should we talk in here?"

Suki watched Michiko walk down the hall. Her roommate kept one eye over her shoulder on Suki as she went along.

Miss Kusawa walked through the doorway. "Certainly Suki, but can we make it quick? I have to change my clothes before the next class."

"Don't worry... " Suki assured her as she pulled the door

closed behind her and locked it. A smile crossed the girl's lips. "We will be finished very quickly."

Miss Kusawa turned to Suki and leaned against the desk. "It's good to see you Suki. What can I help you with?"

"It's about my… boyfriend."

"I was meaning to ask you if you told him about your baby?"

"No, not yet." Suki moved from the door and slowly made her way to front of the classroom.

"Why not? Are you afraid he won't understand?"

"I'm afraid he'll leave me for the other woman."

"She's back? It's been a while. I thought she might be gone for good."

"I had hoped so too, but when I returned from the market today, she was with him in our house." Suki casually clutched her forearm and drew her finger along the desks as she spoke, keeping her head down with her damp hair obscuring her face. "She was in our room. Where only I should be."

"I'm sorry Suki. If there's anything I can do…"

"I saw her face today!" Suki abruptly raised her head and spoke like she had just learned some wonderful news. Her eyes stared wide through matted forelocks. "I know who she is." She came up to the front and stood an arms length from Miss Kusawa: within striking distance. "What should I do about her? I want your advice."

Miss Kusawa was fidgeting uncomfortably. "Do you think she's romantically involved with him?"

"The first time she came out in his robe, her hair was wet…" Suki cocked here head looking at Miss Kusawa's wet hair.

Miss Kusawa made a gesture towards her own hair and looked a little frightened.

"…as if coming out of a bath, and then she kissed him. Michiko saw it with me. She wore his robe. I know, because I've worn it a few times myself. Today, he held her around the shoulder as he walked her out and she gave him… a kiss."

"Ahem, was it a passionate kiss or a friendly one?" Miss Kusawa asked, clearing her dry throat and trying to maintain her composure.

"Does it matter?"

"It might help to determine if it was a friendly encounter or a romantic one. Maybe it was his ex? He may be on good terms with her. Many divorced people are."

"Very good terms, if she bathed at his house and wore his robe."

"Yes, I see what you mean." Miss Kusawa gave a tense smile at Suki's joke.

"Now that I know who she is, I need your advice. What should I do about her? I want her out of our way; she is the last obstacle to our happiness."

"Do you think talking to her would help?"

"She has a boyfriend who probably doesn't know about her affaire."

"an adulterous affaire? Have you confronted your boyfriend about her?"

Suki laughed. "Why? He's a man! Grab his meatstick and he's your puppy! All men are like that. They're slaves to their hormones… and all liars!" She looked up between hairs still dripping from the rain. "This man is my slave and he has one master: ME!"

Miss Kusawa looked fearful by Suki's words and her tone. "Yes, yes, Suki. I understand…"

"YOU UNDERSTAND!" She slammed her hand on the desk. "Then why are you doing this to me!?! Why are you seeing him?" She swung her arm and struck the teacher's face with the back of her hand. "YOU WHORE!" In the state she was in, an adrenaline rush increased her strength.

Miss Kusawa stumbled and fell to the floor next to the desk. She covered the side of her face with her hand, disoriented and shocked by Suki's blow. "Wh-what? Suki! What's wrong with you!"

"You are! Why must you take my man from me?" Suddenly another voice came out of Suki's mouth. "Because you're foreign filth, a baka gaijin who doesn't respect our ways. Thinking you can come in and take our men away from us." Suki straddled Miss Kusawa as she spoke. Then dropped to her knees over her teacher's legs, pinning them underneath her. "Why, I'll just bet that the baby you're carrying is his! Did you lie to Suzuki too, like you lied to me?"

Miss Kusawa was tearful. "Suki, what did I do to make you so angry? Why do you hurt me? That voice… Are you even Suki?"

"What a clever girl to figure it out. I am her mother, her mentor and her soul. Call me Miko, dear."

"Miko!"

"Now that introductions are over and since there can be only one heir to Ted…" Miko removed the knife from Suki's sleeve.

"NO!" Miss Kusawa's screamed as here eyes widened. "What are you going to do with that knife!?!"

Miko calmly said to her, "Well it is a fillet knife. I will fillet your baby and serve it up to you."

Miss Kusawa was now beyond fear as the threat to her unborn child became evident. She gave a scream and a defiant grab at Miko's arm and held the knife at bay. "I won't let you hurt my child – I'll die first!"

Miko cocked her head as she looked at Miss Kusawa. "This isn't a multiple choice test, teacher! But now that you mention it, answer B is as good as Answer A." She shrugged. "Have it your way!" She then used her left fist to punch Miss Kusawa, knocking her unconscious and releasing her grip on Miko's arm. "There's a good girl. You just sleep and it will all be over in a moment."

Touch Me Not

Miko reared her arm back to get maximum thrust.

A blur rushed past Michiko and grabbed the wrist of Miko. It was Mr. Suzuki. He had the key to the room and opened it for her – as it would seem, just in time.

Miko looked up at her arm and saw a hand tightening around her forearm. She looked back to see Mr. Suzuki grapple her arm and holding her shoulder with his other hand. As he squeezed harder, the tendons of her hand relaxed and the knife fell out of her grip. Mr. Suzuki kicked it to the side and spun Miko around.

"Miss Ona! What has come over you? What are you doing?"

"Destroying my rival! She's been with my man. Did she ever tell you about him? No, she hasn't has she."

Mr. Suzuki saw Miss Kusawa on the floor, still dazed by the punch. He threw Miko off of her, and went to her side. He gently picked up her head and rested it in his lap.

"Ayako! Are you all right?"

Miss Kusawa was groggy but lifted her hand to her face. "I-I'm okay. She packs quite a punch for a small woman. Just help me up."

As Mr. Suzuki helped Miss Kusawa to her feet, Miko made her way towards the knife in the corner. As she reached down for it a shoe covered the knife. Looking up she saw Kuno.

"Nope. Not happening."

Then Michiko grabbed Miko's shoulders and pinned her to the wall. "Let her go, Miko! Leave Suki alone!"

"And let her have all the fun with Ted?" She smiled sweetly, then she hissed, "Not a chance!"

Michiko slapped Miko hard. "She's my friend and I won't give her to you! Suki, talk to me, its me, Michiko!"

Suki blinked and looked around the room and then at Michiko. "Michi-Michiko? What's happening? Where am I?"

"You just tried to kill Miss Kusawa!"

"It wasn't me! It was Mommy, it was Miko." She dropped down the wall and huddled into a fetal ball, sobbing.

Miss Kusawa asked. "Who's Miko?"

Michiko left Suki where she was and went to Miss Kusawa. "I'm sorry for not being more truthful to you before, but Suki wanted us to keep her affair secret. She was afraid you wouldn't approve. Miko is the wife of her boyfriend."

"Dead wife." Kuno corrected her.

"Dead wife?" Miss Kusawa looked at Kuno. "Miko is dead?"

Michiko explained, "Yes. Suki learned everything about Miko. Became obsessed with her and now believes that she is in Miko's possession. She developed a split personality, Miko was the one who attacked you, not Suki."

Mr. Suzuki was holding Miss Kusawa around her shoulder. "Well, I've called the police to take them both away!"

A small voice came from the corner. "I can't go back there. They'll take me back and I'll never see my baby. I'll be a bad mother."

Michiko turned to where she left Suki. The girl was panic-stricken.

"I won't go back!" She darted towards the door of the classroom, pushing gawkers out of the way as she ran out.

Michiko called after to Suki. "Come back! We can help you!" She started as if to go after her but Kuno stopped her.

"Stay here, I'll go get her. You have to protect our kids." He smiled at her and moved to the door, taking out his cell phone as he ran.

"Michiko, why didn't you tell me about this before?" Miss Kusawa asked.

"Suki respects you and was afraid that you would disapprove of her boyfriend. She says you would hate him because he's a foreigner and…"

"And, what? Tell me."

"Ted's much older than her." Michiko said.

Miss Kusawa placed her face in hands. Then she removed them and stood up.

"He's fifty-one years old." Miss Kusawa said as she rose from the floor.

"I don't know how old he is, Suki never learned his age."

"I'm not asking you. I'm telling you: Ted is fifty-one."

"How do you know?"

"I'm so, so stupid!   All the clues were right there and I missed them."

"She said you told here that you hate gaijin, like Ted." Michiko said.

"I-I did, once. I resented him for my being an outsider. I held him responsible for all my problems in making friends and finding boyfriends… for my curse. But when I heard what he did for Suki, giving her a job as an intern, I was surprised. I thought about it and decided to visit him to thank him."

"But, that morning, when we saw you in his garden…?" She was interrupted by her cell phone. It was Kuno's ringtone. She answered it. Her face went ashen as the blood drew out of it.

Miss Kusawa moved forward to steady Michiko. "What is it? What's happened?"

"Suki's gone up to the roof." Michiko was shaking. "Kuno thinks she might try jumping off."

Michiko and Miss Kusawa arrived on the roof amid students and campus police. Someone had alerted the local fire brigade: a spotlight lit Suki from below. The rain had returned and Suki stood on the ledge holding on to a pole and trembling.

Miss Kusawa called out to Suki, who didn't seem to hear her amidst the clatter of the rain. She asked the police to let her through so she could talk to her – that she was her teacher. The campus police knew her so they relented. She grabbed Michiko's hand and the two women ran ahead towards Suki, stopping only when she spotted them approaching. Miss Kusawa tried to grab her, but was out of reach. At least she was close enough for them to talk.

"Suki, come down dear!"

"I can't let them take me back there."

Michiko stepped forward. "I know about the home you were put in, Junko. How your family abandoned you. Kuno and I went to your hometown and to your mother, Miko's home. You deserved better!"

"They said I was just cast off, something less than the guts of a fish given to cats. That my mother hated me and threw me away... that I was a bad girl." She looked down towards the ground three stories below. "I can't ever go back there."

"No Junko! You're mother didn't throw you away. She was only a child herself when she had you. Her brother raped her and they took you away from her. She wanted to keep you. You're mother loved you! You'll never go back to that home again." Michiko promised. "You have a family here; Me, Miss Kusawa, Kuno, Mr. Suzuki and Ted. We're your new family and we all love you very much."

Suki looked out into the darkness beyond the horizon, past the buildings and the bright lights shining up at her. "April 15th."

"What's that Suki?" Miss Kusawa asked.

"Michiko once asked me when my birthday is. It's April 15. I know it because every April 15th a woman visited me. She brought me a small cake and a tiny gift each year. She never told me, but I knew she was my mother. On her last visit I asked her name. She said, 'My name is Miko'."

Miss Kusawa stepped forward. "My mother's name was also Miko."

Suki turned here face towards Miss Kusawa. "You!" The voice was distinctly that of Miko. "The home wrecker, the whore, or are you just his mistress?"

"Am I talking to Miko?" Miss Kusawa asked.

"Like I'd ever tell you!"

"Suki, what is Miko's last name?"

"Therioux, what else."

"No, I mean Miko's maiden name?"

Suki hesitated. "It's…"

"You don't know, do you? That's because Miko doesn't know. That's because Miko doesn't exist excepting in your mind."

Michiko tugged at Miss Kusawa's sleeve. "Sensei, I don't think it's a good idea to provoke her."

"I'm not, I'm trying to separate her from Miko long enough to get her down." Miss Kusawa explained. She called to Suki. "Miko! You do not know your maiden name, because you are not Ted's wife! But I do know it! I know your name."

Miko called back. "What are you talking about?"

If you are Ted's wife then you are the mother to his children are you not?

"Of course, you're being stupid."

"What are their names?"

Suki hesitated again.

"All she knows is what you know about her Suki, because you gave her life and believed she really was Miko."

"What do you know?" There was a break in Miko's voice and Suki's came through.

"I know that a mother would never forget the face of her child."

"What… was her name?" It was Suki's voice.

Miss Kusawa stepped forward with Michiko – close enough to grab Suki.

"Her name was Miko… Kusawa. Her children's names are Kenchi and… Ayako. Miko was my mother."

Michiko looked at here teacher, shocked. "Sensei, is it true?"

Miss Kusawa looked apologetically at Michiko and then to Suki, "When my father was accused of killing her, I was ashamed and used her name instead of his when I moved here." She tried to reach out to Suki. "I know about you and Ted! Michiko told me. Suki, you have to know that I am not his lover…"

"But I saw you from the balcony, and today you were there and kissed him."

"Yes, I did that, but it's because…"

Ted's voice came out from the shadows as he stepped forward. "Ayako is my daughter."

"Ted!" Suki said, shocked.

"Father?" Miss Kusawa said looking over at him.

"She heard about my helping you and visited me that night. Since I work late, she fell asleep and woke in the morning as I was doing my daily exercise. I let her use my shower and robe in the morning and she made tea and brought it out to me. She kissed me good morning on the cheek. We talked that all that day and put the past behind us. Thanks to you, she finally forgave me."

A police officer came up to Miss Kusawa and Michiko.

"You have to get her down soon. The storm is producing lightning and she might be struck."

Michiko asked, "Why do you say that?"

He pointed up at Suki. "That's the lightning rod she's clinging to."

Ted reached out for her. "Suki, it was always you that I was with, not Miko. I mourned her, yes, but I know she is dead. You came into my life and brought me more joy than I have felt in years. I love you Suki!"

Suki made a half turn and looked at his outstretched hand, dripping wet from the rain.

After a moment, she reached out for his hand. Moving toward him she lost her footing and slipped back.

Michiko watched her begin to fall and could swear she saw the suggestion of Miko in the raindrops surrounding Suki, her arms around the girl's neck pulling her downwards.

Ted called out. "I have you Suki! Hold on!"

Michiko and Miss Kusawa went to the railing and saw Ted had grabbed her wrist, but with nothing to hold onto she was just dangling there.

Kuno, Mr. Suzuki and two policemen went to help Ted.

Michiko looked down at Suki's scared face, "Hold on Suki! Ted will get you out of this!"

Michiko thought she heard Miko's voice coming out of Suki's mouth. "Well Ted, I wanted to take you with me to my eternal loneliness, but I guess this one will have to do. You took my precious life from me. So, I'm taking away what you love. Bye-bye Ted!"

The flash preceded the boom by milliseconds. The percussive explosion let out a shockwave that knocked down the people standing closest to the lightning rod. Ted struggled to keep his grip on Suki's hand. But Suki was not as strong as Ted.

With that, Suki let go of Ted's hand and fell into the rainy darkness beyond the spotlight.

Bitter Mercy

Suki felt the burning static charge from the lightning strike and the release of her grip from Ted's hand: the tips of their fingers touching for one last time. She perceived Ted's angst-ridden face, frozen in that moment of eternal torment as she began her descent. He was watching someone he loved die before his eyes – for the second time. It saddened Suki as she moved further away from the last of his grip. He had suffered so much in his life that she only wanted to comfort him. It was all she ever wanted for him – happiness. She stared at Ted's face as he disappeared into the gray watery mist.

'Death is beautiful my dear daughter.' Miko's small voice broke through the watery veil to comfort her. 'Embrace it!'

She was aware of a sensation that felt as if she was gliding along, as a soft air stream cushioned her back. Gazing off to her left side, she saw that the rain was no longer falling, but that she was floating among undulating droplets, which seemed like an escort of glittering fairies. She reached out her hand, allowing one of the sparkling fairies to land sweetly on her extended palm, where it bowed to Suki before flying away.

She gazed beyond her palm and saw the sweet smile of Miko, her mother, and heard her say, 'My baby, how I yearn to sing you to sleep now, to stroke your hair and whisper how much I love you.'

Suki thought that if she could just reach a bit farther, stretch out her hand, that she might touch the face of her mother.

'I once went through death and cannot again go through it with you.'

A wash of contentment permeated Suki's breast. The happiness of seeing her mother, hearing her soft voice and feeling her love saturated her soul. Suki smiled.

'Death is something you must do alone.' The small voice trailed off. 'Goodbye for now, my sweet, I will see you soon.'

Miko was gone. Faded into the darkness, abandoning Suki once again: This time to die alone.

She stretched her hand into the watery darkness and felt only the cold. Her tears joined with the glimmering fairies before she lastly laid her head on the soft pillow of death.

"Mommy?"

Epilogue:

Joy

The sound of the breaking waves envelope her: sea spray mists her face and bathes her hair, leaving beads of moisture to tickle sensitive, pale skin. There is the tang of dried salt on her lips as she licks them. The reverberation of the acceding and receding surf is muffled in her ears; it is more of a suggestion than a sound. Warmth coats her face like a pleasant masque; an intense sun shines blazing pink through her closed eyelids. Her feet stand in the surf losing the sand beneath them as the tide ebbs. She digs her toes into the muddy sand to stabilize her stance. Suki's smile twists the edges of her lips upward.

Slowly, carefully cracking open her eyelids, the tropical sunlight blinds her, if only for a brief moment. She focuses her gaze as far away as possible, to where the sea and the sky marry to become one with the horizon. She looks up towards the sky. Perfect clouds gaze back down on her, but there are no birds to interrupt the sounds of the migrating waves. To her right is an island, or is it a peninsula? She cannot know for sure since a low haze obscures much of it.

To her left is the sun, and the reflection of bright morning rays on the water's surface, making it difficult to focus her eyes. There is movement in the shallows of the surf near the beach. At first it seems to be a mirage, wavy heat radiates, with something coming out of it and taking shape. Suki raises her hand to her forehead to better see what is approaching her.

A small child, a little girl, with shiny black hair being tossed about by the breeze, waves, beckoning Suki to come to her. Behind the child a man approaches her and takes her hand. It is Ted. Together with the girl they summon Suki to join them. To the left of the two, on the beach, stands a copse of palm trees, beneath which is a tent sheltering others who are waiting for her. Ayako is there with a child on her lap and Takeshi is standing next to her. She talks to Michiko who sits next to Kuno as he plays with two children – twin boys. Her belly is ripe; she is on the advent of giving birth to another child.

A wave of well-being laps up against Suki. There is a contented joy about this place.

Paradise, it is said, consists of life's bright moments radiating out from the heart and washing away our fears from the dark passages of memory. The moments we choose to embrace – the light or the dark –determines our eternity.

It is perfect.

Suki gazes out to the horizon, turns her face up to the bright sun and she closes her eyes.

They disappear from one another's sight.